Cool Water Justice

Also by Major Mitchell

The Doña

Mokelumne Gold

Poverty Flat

Manhunter

Where The Green Grass Grows

Canyon Wind

A Reason To Believe

Dusty Boots

Joker's Play

Refugio's Gold

Charlie Shepherd (Children's)

The Witch On Oak Street (Children's)

Available now at **www.shalakopress.com**

Cool Water Justice

By Major Mitchell
&
Jerry Mitchell

Shalako Press
P.O. Box 371
Oakdale, CA 95361

ISBN: 978-0-990070-2-0

For information contact: Shalako Press
P.O. Box 371, Oakdale, CA 95361-0371
http://www.shalakopress.com

Cover design: Karen Borrelli
Editor: Judith Mitchell
Cover photograph of Major Mitchell taken by Wiley Joiner

PRINTED IN THE UNITED STATES OF AMERICA

Acknowledgments

Like all books, this book is a combined effort of many people.

We would like to thank Judy Mitchell for her many edits that turn our scribbles into something readable.

We would also like to thank Steve Haak and Gary Crawford for their reviews and for catching additional errors.

A big thanks to historian Wiley Joiner for the photograph of Major Mitchell used on the front cover.

As always, we stop to thank graphic artist Karen Borrelli for creating an attractive cover.

Most of all, hugs and kisses to our families who not only allow, but support our writing habits. We love you.

Dedication

This book is lovingly dedicated to our mother and father, Zula and Clarence Mitchell, who not only gave us a passion for reading, but lived the pioneering spirit we write about.

Cool Water Justice

James Westfall raised his hand in the air and brought his sorrel to a halt. It was a habit he had picked up while leading a band of Confederate gorillas during the war. All three riders dismounted without saying a word. A curl of smoke rose skyward from a clump of mesquite near a small creek. Westfall motioned for Curley to approach the mesquite on his left side, and then motioned for Carlos Mendoza to approach on the right. Both men moved quietly through the dry grass and brush. James waited for a minute before walking quietly toward the smoke.

They had been on the run for the past two days, and he figured they were only an hour, maybe two, ahead of the posse. James had made it an unspoken policy to never admit he'd made a mistake, but the decision to rob the bank at Lehmann's Ranch had certainly proven to be a bad one. But he figured it should have been easy pickings. A simple safe tucked inside a small office in the main ranch house. Besides, he knew Lehmann had just sold a herd of two-year-olds and had been paid off in cash. The safe was loaded.

They had waited until midnight before slipping the lock on the office window. James and Curley crawled through the window while Carlos held the horses quiet. Curley was expert at safe-breaking, especially old ones like Lehmann's. It only took about ten minutes before the last tumbler fell and the door swung open. That's when James heard the creak of the stairs. He quickly blew out the candle and crouched beside the safe as someone passed the office door and down the hall.

"Let's get out of here," Curley whispered.

They quickly stuffed the saddlebags full and were climbing through the window when the dog started barking. Then there were three dogs, charging around the house growling and raising a ruckus. Carlos was having a time simply hanging onto the reins and one of the dogs bit Curley on the leg. He cursed loudly and kicked the animal, then hung onto the saddle horn with one foot in the stirrup as the chestnut bolted down the lane.

Lights came on with shouts coming from the windows as he and Carlos spurred their horses after Curley's mount. Someone came from the bunkhouse and fired a couple of shots and James returned the favor as he rounded the blacksmith's shop and sped out of Lehmann's Ranch. It wasn't until noon the following day that they noticed the posse. They were Lehmann's cowhands, and James knew that every damned one knew how to shoot and were not above hanging a rustler. He figured the same rope would be waiting for them if they were caught.

******

"Hello in the camp," James called as he approached the mesquite. "I smelled your coffee and wondered if you might have a little to share."

"Depends on who's speaking," came a gravelly voice behind the mesquite. "You're welcome to share our coffee and vittles, if you're friendly. If you ain't, well....that might be a different story."

"Friendly? Why, there's folks that claim Jim Westfall is the friendliest guy around."

"Well, show yerself, then."

James stepped into the clearing to see a comfortable camp, well laid out. The speaker happened to be an old grey-headed chap dressed in buckskins. His partners were younger, but James figured by the looks of them, they were well seasoned. The three men had taken positions away from the speaker, leaving plenty of gap between them.

"Y'all look like buffalo hunters," James said.

"Used to be," the old man said with a snicker. "That is, when there was buffalo to hunt. Now, you might say we're something else." He gestured toward the pot with a stick. "Coffee's hot. Help yerself if you got a cup."

"Where's your hoss?" a tall man with shoulder-length hair asked.

"Just right out there," James said, pointing the way he came in. "I got a tin cup in the saddlebag. I'll go get it." He turned, then paused as the tall man pulled his gun."

"Make sure you come back with a cup and nothing else."

"I hear you," James said. That was when Curley's Winchester barked, knocking the tall man forward, where he landed at James' feet. James dove toward the mesquite, pulling his gun as he rolled over. Carlos cut loose with his Henry rifle, hitting one of the other men. James bored the old man through his chest as he pulled a cap and ball revolver from his belt. Curley and Carlos took care of the remaining man.

James stood over the old man and surveyed the campsite. Curley and Carlos appeared, injecting new shells into their rifles.

"That was cutting it mighty close, Curley," James growled. Ya could've waited until I headed toward my horse."

"All I saw was him pulling his iron. I figured the ball was opened, so I sent him to his maker."

"We'd best see what they've got and get moving. Lehmann's posse might've heard the ruckus," James said.

He holstered his .45 and grabbed an empty cup lying by the fire. "But, if'n we're quick, we might have time for a little coffee. Those beans smell mighty good too."

"Their horses look fresher than ours," Carlos said.

"That's what I was hoping for," James said, spooning some beans into a semi-clean tin plate. "You boys grab a plate. No sense letting good grub go to waste. We'll switch horses after we eat. I'll toss my gear onto the chestnut."

"This one only had four dollars and a pack of rolling tobacco," Curley said, rolling the tall man over.

"Well, I ain't figuring they were carrying much. It was their horses and grub I was after." James shoved a spoonful of beans into his mouth. "Best eat while you can, Curley. It might be the last chance you get before we cross the border."

Chapter 2

The prairie schooner creaked as it moved slowly past the sheriff's office. A dog came from the blacksmith's yard and barked, but the oxen plodded forward, ignoring the yapping, and raised small clouds of dust with each step. A handful of people braving the heat of the day only paid cursory attention to the humble parade as they stood in the shade of the awning along the wooden walkway. They were well into their fourth year of an extended drought, and were used to seeing pilgrims leave Texas. The oxen's heads swung back and forth with each step, as though keeping time with unheard music. Clara Jean leaned forward and poked her head from the canvas covering and looked around. She glanced at her husband and shook her head.

"Doesn't look different from any other town we've passed through. What's so special 'bout Carrizo Springs?"

"Nothing, except they've still got water, while the rest of Texas is dried up," Rob said. "At least it did last time I checked." He tapped the left lead ox on the rump with a stick to keep it moving. "Besides, it's only ten miles from Carrizo Springs to Cool Water where my brother's buried." He had walked most of the way from Pittsburg, Texas, and the souls on his boots were well worn.

"Well, that's reason enough, I reckon, but I can't wait to get out of this contraption. Ma and me are 'bout to choke to death on the dust. It hasn't been too pleasant for William either." She sat back and pulled the corner of the sheet back to look at her six-month-old son.

"Yeah, I know. The stable is up yonder on the south end of town. We're almost there, and Teresa's house is real close. She'll let you and ma rest there while we take care of the animals."

The schooner groaned as it maneuvered through a rut in front of the general store. They walked in silence for a minute. Clara's father, Theodore Russell, and her younger brother, Peter, were on the opposite side of the oxen. It was her father who broke the silence.

"Looks like quite a gathering over yonder." He pointed toward a *jacale* sitting twenty yards off the roadway. Rob craned his neck to see over the backs of the oxen. There were a dozen or more gathered in front of the dwelling, including the hulking figure of Marshall Clay Best.

"That's Teresa's house," Rob said. He waited until the schooner had rolled ahead in order to get a better view. He might have thought they were having a party, except for the way Marshall Best kept pacing. The big man didn't look too happy. He stopped his pacing to say something to one of the men, then continued to wear out boot leather. They were close enough now to hear some of the men laughing and talking. Rob guided the schooner toward the *jacale*, when he heard a woman cry out in pain.

"Teresa," he said, "something's wrong with Teresa!" He tossed the ox goad to Peter and dashed toward the *jacale*.

"Hey, help us down," Clara yelled as her husband scampered away.

"Here, hand me Jacob," Hildegarde said, climbing out of the back of the schooner. Clara handed her baby to her mother and jumped to the ground. She marched toward Rob, intending to give him a piece of her mind, when a woman inside the house moaned loudly.

"Best hold your peace and give me a hand," Hildegarde said. "I think we're needed inside. Men are useless at times like this."

"What's wrong, Marshall Best?" Rob asked as he clomped into the clump of men. "Is something wrong with Miss Romero?"

"Wrong? Ain't nothing wrong, boy," A man with a silver star pinned on his vest leaned back in his chair and laughed. "Guess you've been gone awhile. Her name isn't Romero any more. It's Best, and she's having the big lug's baby."

"She's what?"

"Better go help pa and Pete care for the animals while me and ma take care of whoever's inside," Clara said as she brushed past and followed her mother inside.

******

Clay quit his pacing long enough to take a pull on the bottle of tequila Sheriff Ray King had been nursing, then gasped as the fire trickled down his throat.

"Better go easy on that," Sheriff King said with a chuckle, "or you won't be in any shape to greet your son when he arrives."

Clay handed him the bottle.

"What if it's a girl?" Roy Johnson asked. He had closed the blacksmith shop in order to watch Clay suffer. He figured if Teresa delayed giving birth much longer, Clay would give himself an ulcer.

Clay quit pacing and stared at the door as his wife moaned loudly. "Doc Phillips should be here."

"Wasn't any way he could've known she'd go into labor the minute he left town," Ray said. "And I doubt ol' Ben wanted to get a case of the runs and pass it to his entire family. Doc will be back soon enough. She's fine," Ray added as Clay continued his pacing. "Maria's in there, and she's been down that road giving birth to the boys. So's those other women. By the way, who are they anyways? I don't recall seeing them before."

"Reckon you didn't unless it was Rob Mayfield. That's the young feller who ran up asking 'bout Teresa. You recall me telling you about Bill Mayfield getting hisself killed while robbing the bank at Cool Water?"

"Yeah, some." Ray nodded.

"Well, Rob's his brother. He showed up after Billy got hisself all shot to hell by the Lippert brothers. They also killed one of my deputies before I could put an end to it. Anyways, Rob was kinda buggered up when he rode into town. Seems he'd tried stopping his brother from holding up the bank, and Billy took exception to it."

"Too bad he didn't listen to his brother," Roy said.

"I reckon. Anyway, I got a letter from Rob 'bout three weeks ago saying he'd gotten married, and the drought had dried up their farm. They were packing up and moving to California, and he hoped to stop by Cool Water and say goodbye to his brother. He said the whole family was coming, and I guess he wasn't fooling."

Clay turned at the sound of voices to see Rob and his father-in-law approaching, then jerked back around as Teresa cried out loudly. He started toward the door then froze at the sound of a baby's cry.

"You have a beautiful daughter, *Señora* Best," Maria's voice floated through the opened window.

"Hell, now's the time to celebrate," Ray said hoisting the bottle of tequila.

"Here, here," Roy said as he lifted a bottle of whiskey. "To the young lady inside." He took a swig and passed the bottle to Rob's father-in-law. "With Clay as her daddy, she'll need all the help she can get."

"Amen to that," Ray said with a chuckle, then pitched the bottle of tequila to Rob.

Chapter 3

"What I can't figure is how come someone as ugly as you can have such a pretty baby," Ray said, staring at the baby in Clay's lap. The big man only smiled. He was holding the sleeping child as though he thought she would break.

"You should know, since you have two beautiful sons," Maria said as she handed Teresa a cup of water.

"You're not insinuating I'm as ugly as this lug, are you?"

"No, I'm just saying every one of you are drunk. Shame on you, drinking while this woman was bringing a life into the world." She motioned with her head toward Clay as Teresa handed her the empty cup.

"Especially you, *Señor* Clay. You shouldn't be holding her in your condition.

"Well, I can't say I shouldn't have tipped the bottle with these yahoos, but I'm far from drunk." He looked up with a crooked grin. "Question is, is Rob in any condition to make the introductions? You ain't used to drinking, are you, boy?"

"I think that's the first drink of hard liquor he's had," Theodore said with a chuckle.

Rob was seated with his elbows resting against the table. He leaned forward as he talked.

"That's Clara Jean, my wife," he slurred and pointed. "And that's Hildegarde Russell, her ma. This is Theodore Russell, her pa, and this is Pete, her brother."

"Rob Mayfield," Clara said with a scowl. "You are so drunk you forgot to introduce your son." She held the baby up as though she were displaying a trophy. "This is William Mayfield, and he's six months old."

"I don't recall Rob denying he was feeling the effects," Theodore said. "That's what he gets mixing whiskey and tequila. Sort of like tossing a match to a bucket of coal oil."

"Well, I'll whip up some vittles," Hildegarde said. "Maybe some food will sober you men up."

"No need to do that, ma'am," Clay said. "Miguel and Juanita over at the stable said they're fixing supper for everyone tonight."

"Really? Well we'd best fix something for ourselves anyway," Hildegarde said, washing her hands in a pan of water. "We added four mouths by showing up unexpected."

"No, *señora*," Teresa said with a grin. "Juanita knows you are here. There will be enough food for everyone."

"I don't see how she would know."

"They just know," Clay said softly. They're right next door and they're stabling your oxen and horses. Besides, it wouldn't make any difference anyway. Juanita always cooks enough to feed Grant's army."

"That is true," Teresa said. "Now, may I hold my daughter? It is time for her supper."

"Well," Theodore said shuffling toward the door. "I reckon that's our cue to get some fresh air."

Clay passed the baby to Hildegarde and stared at Rob. "Reckon you can make it, or do you need some help?

"I'm okay."

It took three tries before he could scoot away from the table and stagger out the door.

******

Hildegarde helped set the table and agreed that Teresa had not exaggerated about the amount of food Miguel and Juanita would deliver. Dinner arrived in a small buckboard, and Miguel and his family stayed for the festivities. Besides the hot tortillas, beans, spicy pork and rice, several other families appeared with dishes ranging from fried chicken to two barrels of beer from the cantina. She sat on the porch with a plate of pork and fried chicken, watching young *señoritas* and teen-aged boys dance to the strumming of guitars and violins. The music and singing lasted well into the night. She wasn't surprised the following morning to see several revelers passed out in the yard and snoring loudly. She climbed out of the schooner into the crisp morning air and stepped over a rotund man sprawled in front of the door. She crept quietly into the *jacale* to check on the mother and baby.

"*Buenos días, Señora* Russell. How are you this morning?" Teresa was sitting up in bed holding the baby to her breast. Clay rolled over and opened one eye.

"I'm doing just fine, Mrs. Best. That's more than I can say for the bunch scattered across your yard. How's your husband fairing?

"Outside of having one king-sized headache, I'm doing okay." Clay raised himself on one elbow to stare at his daughter, sucking on Teresa's breast. "Hey, take it easy. That's my job."

Teresa gasped and shoved Clay, landing him on the floor. The baby started crying, and she directed it back to her breast. "Please excuse my husband. He has no manners."

Hildegarde laughed as Clay crawled to sit on a wooden chair. "That's quite alright. Perhaps I need to make some coffee."

"Coffee sounds real good, ma'am," Clay said, holding his head with both hands.

Hildegarde leaned over the bed to get a better view of the baby. "By the way, what did you name her?"

Teresa tilted her head toward the baby and smiled.

"Yolanda Elena Maria Rosetta Best."

"That's quite a mouthful. Why so many names?"

"Elena is for my mother. Yolanda is for my grandmother. Maria and Rosetta are for my sisters. I should have more for my godmother and my sister's daughter, but that would be too many names, I think."

"You're right. I think it would be easier to have more daughters, That way you could spread the names out a little. Where do you keep the coffee?"

"In the cabinet by the wash basin." Teresa pointed toward the crude box that looked like it had been built using old apple crates. "Rob has been here before. He can show you where things are. Oh, and tell him I would like him to make *nopales*. He will know what to do."

"Okay, that is good to know," Hildegarde said with a nod. Don't worry about a thing except taking care of that baby. I'll fix coffee first, then see if my son-in-law is able to stand."

She stepped out into the bright Texas sunlight and paused long enough to shove the rotund man with her foot. "Hey, find yourself another place to sleep it off."

"Wha...?" He rubbed a grimy hand across his face and stared at her through blurry eyes.

Hildegarde drew a bucket of water from the well and filled the coffee pot before building a fire in the outdoor stove. She washed her face and hands in the pan hanging on a nail, then marched toward the prairie schooner wondering just how well Rob knew the pretty woman holding the baby, and if there was something he had not told them.

******

Clara Jean stepped into the cool shade of the *jacale* and waited for her eyes to adjust. Teresa was seated on the edge of the cot rocking and singing softly to her daughter. She smiled at Clara, patting the cot next to her.

"Come, *Señora* Mayfield. We have not had a chance to get acquainted."

Clara crossed the dirt floor and sat beside her. She stared at Teresa then hung her head, pretending to study her son.

"What is the matter, *señora*? You look sad. Did those men outside say something to offend you?"

"Wrong? No, nothing like that," Clara said shaking her head.

"Then, what is it?"

"Well, this might sound silly, but you're even more beautiful up close than I thought. Well...I just...feel so...you know," she shrugged her shoulders, "around you."

"Oh, no *señora*," Teresa grabbed her arm. "You are a very beautiful woman and Rob loves you more than anything. He told me."

"He did?"

Hildegarde stepped inside and paused. "Oh, I'm sorry. Looks like I interrupted something."

"No, no," Teresa motioned for her to come closer. "It seems your daughter has some questions you should hear."

Hildegarde grabbed a wooden chair and sat facing the two women. "Okay, what am I supposed to hear."

"I was telling *Señora* Mayfield her husband loves her very much, and that he told me."

"He did? And when did this happen?" Hildegarde asked.

"*Sí,* many times. He came and stayed here in my *casa.*" Her baby woke and started crying. Teresa promptly bared a breast and began feeding her.

"That's what I was afraid of," Hildegarde said, as Clara held her own child to her breast.

"What, that Rob stayed a few days in my *casa*?"

"Frankly, yes."

"*Porque*? There was nowhere else. His brother was at the *cantina* gambling. Where would you have him stay? On the street?"

"There's a hotel right in the middle of town." Clara's voice cracked and she looked away.

"Ah, I think I see. People who stay at the hotel have things missing from their room." Teresa gently grabbed Clara's chin, forcing her to look at her. "*señora*, you have nothing to worry about. Your husband slept in this bed, and I slept in the cot against that wall," she pointed at the cot under the rear window, "with my grandmother. We were friends, not lovers."

"Honest?"

"*Sí*," Teresa said with a nod. "He helped me by fixing the gate and some other things that were broken, and I cooked and washed his clothes. I taught him how to make some Mexican dishes. He is a very good cook. We talked of opening a restaurant, but his brother came and took him away." She shrugged. "He told me about the beautiful Clara Jean he was going to marry. He loves you very much, *señora*."

"Wow! That's hard to believe. You are so beautiful, and I'm..."

"You are pretty also, *señora*." She paused to cover her breast and began burping her baby. "Your husband loves you, not me. Besides, I love my *marido muy fuerte*."

"Your what?" Clara asked.

"My very strong husband. Clay Best is my strong husband, friend and lover. I don't deserve him, and I love him so much. We are both lucky women, *señora*. Don't be jealous of me. Enjoy your family and raise many strong sons for your husband."

******

"But *señor*, the pork is fresh. I killed the pig this very morning." The sweaty butcher paused to wipe his face on the soiled apron he was wearing. It wasn't quite noon and the sun was already beginning to cook everything in sight.

"Look, the pig that roast was taken from was killed sometime yesterday, if it was lucky," Rob said with a scowl. Clara backed away from her husband and cringed. She grabbed a few *jalapeño* peppers and tossed them into the wicker basket belonging to Teresa.

"Look," Rob said as the grocer glared. "Teresa just had her baby, or she'd be down here herself."

"Teresa? *Señora* Best?"

"Yes. I'm going to cook for her tonight, and I don't want to poison her with tainted pork."

"But *señor*, why didn't you say you were buying for *Señora* Best. Wait right here." He disappeared into the back room of the open-air market and returned with a hunk of pork lying on butcher paper.

"This is from the pig I killed just this morning."

Rob studied the roast, rolling it over twice, then nodded. "I can believe you did kill it this morning. We'll take it."

He paid for the meat and the items in the basket, then walked arm-in-arm with Clara Jean back toward the *jacale*. Clara cleared her throat after a minute and shook her head. "What was going on back there? I've never see you act that way."

"What was going on was, he was trying to sell me a hunk of spoiled meat. That roast would've made everyone sick."

"Well, it's good you know something about buying unspoiled meat," she said with a nod and giggle. "You just took me by surprise. Is it true you and Teresa discussed opening a restaurant?"

"Yes, but it was more her idea than mine. I knew we'd be moving on as soon as Bill got tired of playing or got run out of town. As it turned out, helping Teresa with her restaurant would've been a whole lot safer than robbing banks. Too bad he didn't listen. He still might've been alive."

"There ain't no way your brother would have been caught dead working in a restaurant," Clara said with a laugh.

"Yeah, I reckon you're right," Rob said as they turned off the road into Teresa's yard. Clay was sitting on an empty crate in the shade of an umbrella tree smoking his pipe and talking to Clara's father and brother. Peter was sitting on the ground petting Antonio. The large mongrel seemed to be enjoying the attention.

"That's the first time I've seen anyone besides Teresa get that close to him without getting a hunk bit out of them," Rob said.

"Oh, I've given him a pat or two, but I wouldn't recommend anyone else trying it," Clay said. "I hear you're fixin' vittles tonight. What are we having?"

"Chile verde. You might want to go to the cantina and pick up a bucket of beer. I didn't think to buy any."

"Now, that's an idea," Clay said, standing and stretching his back.

"I didn't mean right now," Rob said. "I've still got to cook it, and that'll take most of the afternoon."

"There's no law against sampling the goods before you buy, is there? Come on Ted, let's leave these young folks to their cooking."

"Come to think of it, I do feel a thirst coming on," Theodore said.

"Not you," Clara said as Pete started to follow the men. "You get to stay and clean up behind us."

******

"I'm going too," Teresa said. Clay had been saying that he would take Rob and the Russel family to Cool Water so Rob could visit his brother's grave before leaving to California.

"No, you ain't. You just had a baby," Clay said with a growl.

"Yes, I had our baby. I am not an invalid," she snapped. "And I'm not going to sit here alone in this house, while you are going all over Texas." She waved her hands in the air and glared back.

"Besides," she continued, "Julio and Manuel Rosales and their wives do not even know I've given birth."

"Oh, as fast as news gets around this burg, I'm sure they've heard by now," Clay said. Then pointing a finger at her he added, "You ain't going, and that's that."

Theodore and Hildegarde both laughed as Teresa grabbed a soggy diaper from a basket on the floor and threw it at her husband.

"Y'all ain't been married very long, have you?" Hildegarde asked.

"A couple months past one year," Clay said. "Why?"

"It's pretty obvious," she said with a nod. "You still think you can boss her around, and Teresa still thinks she can do most anything she wants without asking your permission. I figure you'll both mellow, given another year or so .... if you don't kill each other first."

"You'd best let her go, or you'll never hear the end of it," Theodore said with a chuckle.

Chapter 4

Carnie dismounted and surveyed the carnage.

"There's another one over here," Rusty yelled.

"Dammit!" He cursed and kicked the empty coffee pot. "How long do you think?"

"Hard to say. One hour, maybe more. The ashes are still warm," Montana said, poking the campfire with a stick.

Carnie cursed quietly as he turned in a slow circle. The makeshift posse was made up of Lehmann ranch hands. Only one of them, Rusty, had ever done anything like this, and that had been several years earlier. Not that any of them were afraid of a fight, but Carnie figured they should have caught them by now.

"From the smell, I reckon these guys were buffalo hunters. This one's got a skinning knife," Roberto said.

"Buffalo?" Montana said with a shrug. "There ain't none around here that I know of."

"What do you want do now, Carnie?"

"I'd like to catch and hang the sons-of-bitches, but I reckon these men deserve a decent burial."

"The law should be notified somehow," Rusty said. "It ain't just robbing now. We've got four dead men here."

"And what do you suppose we should do?"

"If it was me, I'd toss them on those horses and take 'em into Carrizo Springs. It's maybe ten, twelve miles from here."

Carnie glanced around once more.

"I reckon you're right. Those horses are pretty played out, and can't go much farther than that."

He pulled the makings out of his shirt pocket and rolled a cigarette.

"We'll spend the night in Carrizo Springs and rest the horses. Then," he paused to light the smoke, "we'll head back to the ranch. We'll let the law catch and hang 'em."

Chapter 5

James Westfall, Curley Hammond and Carlos Mendoza rode the stolen horses into Carrizo Springs from the north about an hour after Clay had escorted Rob and his family out of town south toward Cool Water and headed straight for the saloon. Westfall let the batwing doors swing shut behind him, then stepped aside as his two partners entered seconds later. A crooked grin crept across his face as he recognized the man behind the bar.

"Charlie Roberts! What in the hell are you doing here? Get tired of pushing Les' rot-gut whiskey?"

"Not exactly, Westfall. Les Bishop got hisself killed by a bunch of Apaches."

"The hell you say," Curley said.

"Sure as you're standing there," Charlie said as he finished drying the mug he'd been working on and leaned against the bar with both hands. "What can I get for you gentlemen? Cold beer?"

"You read my mind," Westfall said. "Does it taste any better than the goat piss you sold at Cool Water?"

"That was Les' idea," Charlie said with a snicker. "He bought it because it was the cheapest he could find."

He topped off a mug and passed it to Westfall and started filling a second.

"This is real beer kept on ice. What do you think?"

"Damn, that's good," Westfall said, then finished draining his mug.

"Yeah, them Apaches killed and scalped ol' Les and tied him to a wagon wheel. Marshal Best found his carcass a few hours after they'd finished." Charlie finished filling Carlos' mug, then reached for Westfall's mug. "Another?"

"Damn straight," Westfall said, slapping several double eagles on the counter. "Give me a bottle and three glasses also, and let me know when that starts getting low."

"Who's running Cool Water now, that pretty granddaughter of his?" Curley asked.

"No, Marshall Best got remarried, and he and his new wife, Teresa, bought the ranch from Ruth. They've got plans to rebuild it, once the drought lets up. It'll be a hell of a job." He said with a chuckle. He placed a bottle of whiskey and three shot glasses on the counter. "The Apaches burned most everything except the saloon."

The three men laughed as they took their beers and bottle of whiskey to an empty table near the far corner of the bar. Charlie poured beers for two men at the far end of the bar then pulled a small tablet from under the counter and began scribbling a note. He tore the page from the tablet, folding it several times, then wrote *Ray King* on one side. He took it through the door at the back of the saloon and into the kitchen. Finding the young Mexican dishwasher, he placed the note in his palm.

"Go out back and take this to the sheriff's office. Don't stop or talk to anyone. Make sure you give this to Sheriff King personally. Got that?"

"*Sí, Señor* Charlie." The lad dashed through the rear door to the kitchen and disappeared.

Charlie went back to the bar and announced loudly, "For those who are interested, the cook will be ready to serve hot tortillas with beef and chili here in a few minutes."

"Hell, I think he'll be havin' to cook more when we get our hands on the pot," Westfall roared loudly.

Charlie went back to serving drinks and cleaning the bar. James Westfall polished off his beer and leaned across the table.

"Carlos? Once you're finished with your beer, you'd best take them horses to the livery. You'll find it right at the end of town, that-a-way." He pointed toward the south. "See if the Mexican who runs it has any fresh ones he's willing to swap for. We've still got a good twelve or thirteen miles to the Rio."

"*Sí, Jefe.*" Carlos downed the remaining beer and rose from the table.

"*Gracias amigo.* We'll have a fresh beer waiting when you get back."

Westfall watched the vaquero disappear before pulling the cork on the whiskey bottle. It was almost twenty minutes later when the batwing doors swung open and shut. Westfall looked up with blurry eyes, expecting to see Carlos approaching their table. Instead, it was a tall man wearing a badge and carrying a shotgun.

"The name's Ray King, in case you're wondering. I got myself a wanted poster back at the office that says the both of you are wanted for several bank robberies. I want you both to keep both hands in sight and stand up. Then, I want you both to drop your gun belts on the floor. Now!" he added as they stared at him.

Both men slowly scooted their chairs away from the table as a familiar figure peered over the batwing doors.

"Ray, behind you!" Charlie yelled, but it was too late. Ray King was propelled forward as Carlos pulled the trigger. Ray hit the floor with a moan and lay face-down, not moving.

Westfall turned toward Charlie with his gun drawn.

"You miserable snake. We come in here peaceful-like, thinking you're our friend."

"I am, Jim .... I am."

Westfall pulled the trigger, and Charlie slammed into the liquor cabinet behind the bar before falling from sight. Westfall reloaded his pistol and downed the glass of whiskey.

"We'd better go, *amigo*," Carlos said. "This town, it has a lot of people, and they will be coming. I brought some horses from the stable."

"Yeah, let's hit the trail."

Westfall jammed the cork back into the bottle and headed toward the door, stopping long enough to scoop some loose money from the bar. Curley and Carlos both drained their shot glasses and followed. Westfall was staring at the three non-descript animals tied to the hitching rail.

"That was the best they had," Carlos said, mounting a brown mustang with a white blaze between its eyes.

"Let's hope they make it to the Rio and into Mexico," Westfall said, mounting a dun.

All three men spurred the animals and galloped south out of town.

Chapter 6

The surrey slowed to cross a creek bed containing a trickle of water, then rolled to a stop. Hildegarde set the brake and stared at what was left of Cool Water, Texas. A stable that sported a well-used corral and a small adobe structure sat twenty yards to their left. Smoke curled in the air from two young women cooking over an outdoor stove in front of the adobe cabin. A saloon with gray weathered siding stood a hundred yards ahead on the right side of a wide dirt road. The charred foundations of a dozen or more buildings of various sizes lay scattered on both sides of the road. At the far end of the town site stood one weathered cabin adjacent to a cemetery. Two new cabins were currently under construction, but as far as she could tell, that was the extent of Cool Water, Texas.

"It doesn't look like much," Teresa said quietly, causing Hildegarde to burst out laughing.

"No, it doesn't. I can agree with you there."

"That is Julio Garcia and Leo Santiago working on a new *casa*," Teresa said, gesturing toward two men shoveling dirt onto a sod-roofed cabin. "Their wives are cooking at the stable."

Clara climbed out of the surrey and spun in a slow circle, shielding her eyes against the sun as she clung to her baby with one arm. She shook her head and laughed as Rob dismounted and joined her side.

"I can't believe you made us come all the way out here, for this." She waved her arm in an arch.

"This is where Billy is buried," he said quietly.

"Yeah, but you could've rode out here by yourself and left the rest of us back in Carrizo Springs."

"You knew Billy."

"Yeah, and I didn't really like him. I didn't mean it like that," she added as he turned away. "What I mean was, there ain't no place to spend the night. Where are we gonna sleep?"

"You can sleep in my husband's old casa with me and your mother," Teresa said. "It's there." She pointed toward the cemetery."

"It looks haunted."

"Not since I had the priest bless it. I feel June's spirit sometimes, but she has a kind soul."

"June?" Hildegarde asked.

"*Señor* Clay's first wife. She was sick and died." Teresa held her baby firmly against her breast as she walked briskly toward one of the new cabins.

"Did she die inside the cabin?" Clara yelled.

"*Sí*, but there's nothing to be scared of. As I said, June was a kind soul."

"Lord, have mercy," Clara said, turning a worried face toward her mother. "Where's daddy?"

"Oh, your pa stopped back yonder," Hildegarde pointed the way they had come. "Don't ask me what they're up to."

Clara craned her neck to see her dad and brother listening to Clay talk about something as he pointed toward a lot of open land.

Clay had reluctantly allowed Teresa to make the trip, as long as the women rode in the surrey, and had also insisted on packing two-days' worth of food into the back of the surrey. She had argued, wanting to ride her horse Diablo. But seeing her husband's stern glare, she gave in after calling him several names in Spanish. Clara asked Clay later what she had said, and all Clay would say was, "You don't want to know."

Julio Garcia had seen them coming from the sod roof of the cabin he was building for Estrella and climbed down the ladder. They had been married six months, and while she hadn't said anything, he had a gut feeling a child might be coming. He grabbed his shirt and fastened the buttons as Leo Santiago jammed his shovel in the ground.

"Who do you think they are?" Leo asked as the women waited for the men to join them.

"I guess *Señora* Best will tell us," Julio said as Teresa joined them.

"*Señora*," Both men said with a slight bow.

"Julio, Leo," Teresa said. "This is my daughter," she pulled back the corner of the thin blanket to allow the men a peak.

"She is very beautiful, just like her mother," Leo said.

"*Gracias*," Teresa said. "You remember me telling you both about my friend, Rob Mayfield?"

"*Sí*," both men said with a nod.

"That is him at the cemetery, visiting his brother's grave. The young woman with the baby is his wife, and the others are her family. They are farmers and know how to grow things. I want you to help me talk them into staying. If we are to live here, we will need something besides cattle to eat."

******

"So, what interesting thing did you men find to discuss?" Hildegarde asked as Theodore sat beside her on the homemade bench. They had unpacked the surrey and stored the food inside the adobe cabin to keep cool. Theodore placed two hot corn tortillas on her plate of beef and beans.

26

She couldn't help feeling that the two women cooking had somehow known they were coming, judging from the amount of food they had prepared. "You certainly spent enough time out by that wash talking."

"Clay was just explaining his plans for this ranch. He's got a little over a thousand acres here."

"That's a fair piece of land," Hildegarde said. "I'm guessing they'll need more than the six of them."

"*Sí*," Teresa said. "We plan to hire some *vaqueros*, but I was hoping to talk all of you into staying."

"What," Hildegarde said, choking back a laugh.

"There ain't no way," Clara said, glaring at Rob.

"Why?" Hildegarde asked.

"Because, when we hire *vaqueros*, we will need to feed them, and you know how to grow food."

Hildegarde and Ted stared at Teresa. It was Ted who cleared his throat and laid his fork back in the plate.

"Well, I can't argue with your logic, young lady. But I was hoping to buy my own spread once I got to California."

"*Sí*, but California is a long way. It'll take you months to travel there, and it will be very hot and dangerous. Stay here, and we will build you a nice *casa*, and we'll build one for Rob and *Señora* Mayfield also. They can raise a nice family right here." Teresa leaned forward with a pleading expression.

"As I said, there ain't no way I'm living way out here. There ain't nothing but cactus, snakes and dirt," Clara said.

"Well, I hope you're not thinking we're gonna leave it this way," Clay said with a chuckle. Them two cabins are just the beginning. I can see a dozen or more houses, a general store and a schoolhouse. We've all got young-uns to care for, and I don't plan on having ignorant folks living here. I'm looking to have a nice ranch, once this drought lifts."

"I agree you've got a nice place here," Ted said, taking a fork-full of beef. He chewed for a couple of seconds. "But the fact still remains, I'm hoping to have my own spread."

"We will sell you part of Cool Water, if you stay," Teresa said.

Hildegarde laughed and shook her head.

"From the look on his face, I think you ought to discuss that with your husband before promising to sell a chunk of land."

"Well, it ain't such a bad idea," Clay said after Leo and Julio quit laughing. "We've done much the same thing with these *vaqueros*. They're part owners in the ranch, and as it grows, so will their profits. I reckon we can work out much the same deal, if you're interested." He took a bite of tortilla and beans, then chewed and swallowed. "We'd best sleep on it and make up our minds in the morning."

Clara squeezed Rob's arm and glared in his face. "I'm telling you there ain't no way I'm staying here."

Chapter 7

Clay was sipping his first cup of morning coffee when he saw them coming. He rose slowly from the wooden crate he'd been using as a stool and set the tin cup aside. Teresa looked up from the sizzling frying pan to shade her eyes.

"What is it?" she asked as Julio joined Clay's side.

"Can't be good, whatever it is. It'd take something earth-shaking to pry Roy Johnson away from his blacksmith shop this time of day."

"It looks like Miguel with him," Julio said.

"Got trouble?" Theodore asked as the riders drew closer.

"Not directly. More'n likely some doings in town." Clay stepped forward as the two riders stopped and dismounted.

"What brings you out here this time of day, Roy? Need someone to shoe some horses for you?"

"No, we come with some bad news."

"Figures. I didn't think you rode all the way out here for your health. What's up?" Clay said.

"Thank you, ma'am," Roy said as Teresa handed both men a cup of coffee. He took a sip, then cleared his throat.

"Ray and Charlie both got themselves shot yesterday afternoon."

"What? How are they?" Clay asked as Teresa said a quick prayer, crossing her breast.

"Charlie's going to be laid up for a while, but he's doing okay. It's Ray who's in a bad way. Doc says he might not make it."

"Damn!" Clay turned toward Teresa, then turned back just as quickly. "You got any idee who done it?"

"Oh, yeah. Charlie says it was James Westfall and his two friends, Curley Hammond and a Mexican pistolero. They rode out of town right after the shootin'. Folks sent us out here to get you, hoping you'd go after them."

"Westfall!" Clay said the name like a curse word as he checked the loads in his pistol. "I should've killed him when I had the chance."

"Who's Westfall?" Hildegarde asked.

"A very bad *hombre*," Teresa said. "We saw him and his friend pee on God's church. I don't think *Dios* liked it one bit."

"What?" Hildegarde looked at Clay who was checking his Winchester.

"It's true. They were drunk and decided to piss on the wall of the old mission chapel outside of town." He grabbed his saddle and whistled at the large black horse inside the corral. "Loco, get over here."

"Ya'll better eat something first," Theodore said. "Then maybe have the women pack something for the trail."

"I reckon Maria will be needing you," Clay said, tossing the saddle on Loco's back. He paused to stare as both Julio and Leo started saddling their horses.

"One of you two need to stay and look after things. Ain't likely anything bad's gonna happen, but you never know. Especially you," he said to Leo. "You've got a wife and kid to care for."

"*Sí, Jefe.* But so do you," Leo said, tightening the cinches.

"True, but Ray King is my friend, and Julio ain't got any young'uns yet. I'll take Julio this time. You stay and look after the ranch. If you need anything, just sign for it at the store. Lord willing, we shouldn't be gone too long."

******

"The bullet hit an artery, and Sheriff King lost a lot of blood. I stopped the bleeding and stitched him back together, but it's still a guessing game right now." Doctor Michael Spencer was new in town and fairly young. Clay had had his doubts, figuring he might be unexperienced.

"Ray's my friend, Doc." Clay shuffled his feet on the braided rug in Doctor Spencer's living room.

"I understand, Mr. Best. He is mine also. I'll take care of Sheriff King, while you catch the men who shot him. Is that a deal?"

"I reckon it is."

Clay stopped with his hand on the door knob and looked back.

"One thing you can count on, Doc."

"And what's that, Mr. Best?"

"If I find them, I ain't bringing anyone back for you to stitch up."

"I never thought you would. Good luck," he said as Clay opened the door.

Chapter 8

It was late afternoon when Clay returned to Doctor Spencer's house. Maria was seated beside her husband's bed, and from the look of her tear-streaked face, he figured she was on the edge of collapsing.

"I figured you'd be long gone by now," the doctor said quietly.

"We've got a pack horse ready with supplies, and figure to leave at first light. Those yahoos rode out without much more than the shirts on their backs, so they'll be traveling slow. We figure to ride hard, and we should be breathing down their necks in a day or two." Clay studied Ray for a minute before nodding toward Maria.

"The boys are doing fine. Teresa and Mrs. Russell are spoilin' the dickens out of them."

"*Gracias, Señor* Clay. You have been more than kind."

"Nonsense. Me and Ray's rode some dusty trails together, and I aim to finish this one. You just make sure he takes it easy. And tell him I want to see him up outa that bed by the time I get back."

"*Sí,* I will." She turned her attention back to her husband, and began to quietly recite a prayer.

"So," Clay said to the doctor, "how's his chances?"

"About the same as this morning...perhaps a little better. The longer he hangs on, the better his chances for a full recovery. The chore is going to be getting liquid and nourishment into him while he's unconscious."

"Huh," Clay said with a chuckle. "Wave a mug of cold beer under his nose and he'll drink it."

"That's not really such a bad idea," Doctor Spencer said with a chuckle. "There's a lot of calories in beer. I might try it when I think he's able."

"When it comes to vittles, ask Teresa. She'll get him to eat, or she'll pester him until he does, that's for sure."

******

They were eight miles southwest of town when the sun began to peek over the Anacacho Mountains. The rocky hills were sliced with limestone canyons and washes and were dotted with shrubs and cactus, climbing to a height of 1,316 feet. Clay was thankful they were heading away from the mountains, and had always considered the hills a good place to break a horse's leg. Julio climbed back onto his horse and studied the horizon.

"The tracks are headed that way, toward the Rio." He pointed south.

"I was afraid of that. They're heading toward Mexico. Well, that ain't going to stop me none, since I ain't no legal lawman. You got any qualms 'bout crossing the border?"

"No," Julio shook his head slowly. "There are some of the *banditos* and f*ederales* who would not want us there, but, we do what we need to do, *Jefe*."

"That's what I thought. How far are they ahead?"

Julio shrugged. "One day, maybe. They were riding hard, and will have to stop and rest *los caballos*, but there is nothing from here to the Rio Grande. They will have to slow down or kill the horses."

"Well, let's close the gap a little. I want to see Jim Westfall barking in hell before this deal's over."

Chapter 9

Captain Jose Ramos of the fifth regiment *of Los Federales de Mexicanos*, now retired, stared at the dry, baked pasture where the cattle used to graze. The buzzards were getting fat and lazy feeding on the carcasses of the dead animals and the stench was overpowering. He turned his horse and rode slowly toward the hacienda, pausing next to the cornfield. He could remember when the corn towered over his head and produced sweet, tender ears. The drought-ridden plants had not grown past waist-high this year, and were dry and brittle. His dream of retiring on the family farm near Juarez was slowly drifting away with the dust.

His son, Roberto, had a wife and four children to support, and with the drought, the five-hundred acre farm could barely feed them, let alone support Captain Ramos and his wife. They had been living on his meager retirement, but it was never enough, especially with the government haggling and in-fighting in Mexico City. He dismounted at the barn and studied the dusty, sweat-soaked back of his son trying to plow the dry-packed earth with a half-starved, over-worked mule, and choked back a lump in his throat. He turned the horse into an empty stall and walked briskly toward his son.

"Roberto," Jose said, joining his side.

Roberto stopped the mule and wiped his forehead. "*Si?*"

"I was thinking. With the drought, this rancho is not going to support your family with me and your mother living here. I believe it is time for us to find another place to live."

"But, *Padre*, we've always said you would live here when you retired. We enjoy having you and mother here. It's the family rancho."

"*Si*, and any other time, that is what I dream of doing. But it simply isn't possible with this drought. Maybe when the rains come again."

"Where will you go?"

"I don't know. Perhaps California. I understand there is plenty of land and water."

"California is a long way from here, papa. If you go to California, we will never see each other again."

"*Si*, and your mother will not like it. But it is far better than watching my grandchildren suffer and starve."

Roberto unhitched the mule and they walked back toward the barn, leading the tired animal. Jose cringed at the idea of telling Juanita. It would not be pleasant, but the move was needed.

He spent the next three days greasing the wheels on the old buckboard and packing their belongings, while listening to Juanita cry. The dream of having the grandchildren close, even in the same house to wake her in the morning, was not going to die easily. With the wagon loaded, they said their goodbyes and left at daybreak. The dry wooden spokes rattled as Jose walked the horses toward the Rio Grande. A broken wheel was one thing he did not need, especially with Juanita staring quietly at the dusty road ahead. Her cheeks glistened with moisture in the sunlight.

"Here," he said reaching behind the seat to hand her an umbrella. "We have a long way to go. There is no reason to get sunburned on the first day."

An hour had almost passed when he guided the horses into the Rio Grande and stopped midstream.

"Why are we stopping," Juanita asked.

"We need to let the wheels soak up water and tighten the spokes. We'll leave in a few minutes. Would you like something to eat?" He reached for the picnic basket beneath the seat.

"No, thank you. I couldn't eat a bite. I don't know if I'll eat again."

"I know. I feel as if my insides have been ripped out also. I wanted to see my grandsons grow into men and give my granddaughter away in marriage." He pulled a single corn tortilla from the basket and took a bite.

"Then why are we doing this?"

"Because, as we discussed a hundred times, the rancho cannot possibly support us and Roberto's family at the same time."

"But there has to be somewhere closer than California. Isn't there?"

Jose urged the horses a few feet forward and stopped, allowing the other half of the wheels to soak. He tied the reins to the brake and stared thoughtfully into the distance.

"Actually, there might be."

"Really?" Juanita asked, grabbing his arm. "Where?"

"An old friend of mine, Clay Best, was marshal at a place named Cool Water. It's been a year since I've seen him, but he said they still had water ... at least they did a year ago. Cool Water is near Carrizo Springs. Perhaps he might know if there is a place there where I can find work." He looked at Juanita and grinned.

"How would you like seeing your husband sweeping floors inside a store?"

"It would be a lot safer than chasing Apache and banditos." She stared at the road on the opposite side of the river.

"How far is your friend's Cool Water from our son and grandchildren?"

"It would take about three days in a wagon to reach them. Faster by horseback or stage...if there is one that goes to Juarez. I don't know if that is possible."

"That would be better than California."

"Then, it is Cool Water. I can't guarantee anything, but we will try."

Jose waited a few more minutes before starting the wagon forward. The spokes were noticeably quieter when he pulled onto the road and turned east, following the river toward Carrizo Springs. Juanita was right. She had been a good, faithful wife, and supported him while he was an officer in the army. She had spent many lonely nights alone, caring for children and worrying for her husband. She deserved better. His son and grandchildren deserved better He had no idea what he was going to do. Perhaps his friend, Clay Best, might know of a small farm, or some work in town that he could do to support his family.

He grinned and cocked his head to one side as he urged the team into a trot. Perhaps sweeping floors would not be too bad. He wouldn't have to worry about stopping a bullet or an arrow, and could sleep in a warm bed next to his wife.

Chapter 10

James Westfall dismounted and checked the hooves on the dun gelding he'd been riding. The horse had been favoring his left front one for the past half hour.

"*¿Qué es, Jefe?*" Carlos asked.

"Stone bruise." Westfall straightened his back and mopped his face with a sweat-soaked bandana. "It ain't got many miles left before it gives out. Is there any place near where we can get fresh mounts?"

"Not that I'm aware," Curley said, lighting a cigarette. "You know somewhere, Carlos?"

"No, not nearby," he said slowly. "Maybe we camp here tonight and the horse will feel better in the morning."

"Hell, it'd take a good week or more to make this nag feel better," Westfall growled. "Unless you know some miracle cure I ain't aware of."

Carlos took a swallow of water and recapped the canteen.

"I'll soak the hoof and pack it with some dried herbs to bring the swelling down. "Two days would be better, but it should feel better in the morning."

Westfall fumbled around inside his saddlebag for a bottle of tequila. He pulled the cork and took a swig before passing the bottle to Curley.

"We ain't got two days. There has to be some sort of a posse following our trail, and we don't know how far back they are."

He used his hat to shade his eyes and scanned the sky.

"I figure we've got 'bout three hours to sundown. We can make camp here and Carlos can work his magic. You'd better go easy on the water, though. We can't tell if the next waterhole still has water. Curley, climb up that ridge and see if you see anyone before we unsaddle."

Curley grabbed a looking glass from his saddlebags and scampered up a small rise. Lying on his belly, he searched the expanse for several minutes before climbing back down.

"Didn't see nary a soul. I think Lehmann's boys gave up."

"It ain't Lehmann's boys I'm worried about. We plugged the sheriff in Carrizo Springs and Charlie Roberts. If you think 'bout it, they both were friends of Clay Best. Him and that Mexican friend of his...what's his name?"

"Julio Garcia?" Curley asked.

"Yeah, it's them two I'd be worried about." Westfall took another pull on the bottle of tequila.

"Clay Best? You ain't scared of that old man, are you?" Curley asked with a chuckle.

"Scared, no I ain't scared." Westfall turned away, but turned back just as quickly to point a finger in Curley's face. "I ain't scare of no one."

"Take it easy, Jim," Curley said, holding both hands up in surrender. "I know you're not scared of anything that I know of. I just figured you'd want to brace that old goat to settle things."

"I plan on doing that someday. But we need better horses than what we got, 'cause these are about done in." Westfall pitched Carlos the bottle and sat cross-legged in a sandy area to roll a cigarette.

"I wouldn't mind having that big black horse of his when this is all over. You can have that red horse of Teresa's if you want."

"Forget the horse," Curley said with a laugh. "I'll take her."

"Yeah," Westfall said with a snicker. "The thing is," he paused to light his smoke, "we've both seen him kill too many men not to respect his gun hand. And bracing Clay Best and Julio Garcia both, way out here with lame horses, ain't my idea of staying healthy."

He stretched his long body in the sand to enjoy his smoke. Carlos gathered a couple of handfuls of dry leaves and bound them to the horse's hoof with a bandana and soaked it with water from his canteen.

"You think that'll really work?" he asked.

"Maybe," Carlos said with a shrug.

"I hope so," Westfall said and tossed his cigarette butt away. He closed his eyes and let his sunbaked brain wander. Curley was right, he did have a score to settle with Clay Best, and it didn't matter how tough the old buzzard was. There was an old wound inside his gut that had been festering for two years now, and it needed taking care of.

He replayed the scene over in his mind, recalling every detail. He and Curley had ridden into Cool Water, looking for a place to hang out while things cooled down. What happened in Austin wasn't much, in his mind, but the law took a dim view of him killing a two-bit cardsharp called Lew Diamond. Folks who knew Diamond knew he was a cheat and figured he'd gotten what he had coming. But the law didn't figure it that way, and they had ridden out of town minutes before being arrested.

They spent most of their time in Cool Water inside the saloon, drinking and playing cards with Les Bishop, owner of the Cool Water Ranch, and everything attached. That included the bank, saloon, livery, general store and the cattle roaming over the thousand acres of grassland. It didn't take long for Westfall and Curley to realize that Les believed he owned the souls of those living and working on the ranch, including his pretty teenage granddaughter, Ruth. But Les' favorite pastime was drinking whiskey and playing cards. It didn't take long to win the old man's trust. All they had to do was sit at Les' table, buy a couple of drinks, and loose a few dollars playing cards. Ol' Les didn't catch on when his luck turned and Westfall and Curley started winning more than they lost. Soon, he was in debt up to his ears.

That particular morning, town marshal, Clay Best, had returned from chasing a couple of rustlers off the ranch, to discover his wife, June, had died. Not only had June Best died, but Les Bishop had ordered her to be buried in the small cemetery. He claimed no one knew when Clay would get back into town, and her body certainly wouldn't keep more'n a day or two at the best. She'd been in the ground a full day when Clay rode into town.

Westfall and Curley were seated at Les' favorite table drinking and playing cards at the time, and heard the big man bellow like a bull when he discovered his wife was gone. Westfall could see him bursting through the saloon doors, almost tearing them from the hinges, cursing a blue streak. Les told him to calm down and he'd explain what happened, but Clay wasn't having any of it. That's when Westfall had made a real horseshit mistake.

"What the hell, Clay? She was a lunger, and she's better off dead."

Clay kicked Westfall's chair out from beneath him and flung the table on its side. Westfall had grabbed for his gun as he came up from the floor, but a hard right hand from Marshal Best caught him on the jaw, knocking him back to the floor. His gun slid across the floor, and Westfall shook the cobwebs from his head as he scrambled on all fours toward the weapon. That's when Clay brought his size 14 boot down on his gun hand, causing Westfall to holler in pain. Clay kicked the gun toward the bar and waited for him to rise to his feet. That's when he began pounding him with both fists. Westfall remembered trying to fight back, but soon discovered Clay Best was quicker than a snake and hit like a mule.

Looking back on it, he figured Clay would have beaten him to death, if Dusty and Utah hadn't drug him from the saloon and forced him to calm down. Even then, he had busted up the saloon real good, smashing several chairs and threatening to shoot Les Bishop.

Westfall opened his eyes and raised to support himself on one elbow.

"Hey, Curley. That day Clay gave me the beating, why didn't you try to stop him?"

"I did. I started to pull my iron and send him to hell, but Utah jammed his .45 against my nose and took my gun. There wasn't anything I could do. Why?"

"Nothing. Just wondering." He lay back down and closed his eyes. "I guess Utah and Dusty were both friendly with the old coot, weren't they?"

"Yeah, reckon they were," Curley said.

Chapter 11

He woke late the following morning to the sound of hushed voices. Curley and Carlos were lying on their bellies on the ridge. Curley was studying something through the binoculars. He passed the glass to Carlos and pointed.

"Hey, what are you guys looking at?"

"Come take a look, but keep it down," Curley said.

Westfall climbed the small ridge and knelt beside Curley.

"Lay on your belly, unless you want to advertise where we are."

"Lehmann's boys?" Westfall reached for the glass.

"Na," Curley shook his head, "but just as bad. Clay, and he's got Julio Garcia with him."

"You sure?"

"Sure I'm sure. Right over there," he pointed, "by them boulders. I figure Lehmann's boys might've given up by now. I ain't for sure, but Clay might have some of those townspeople tagging along."

"Yeah, that's him and Garcia alright," Westfall said, lowering the glass. "I don't figure they've got any townsfolk with them. I reckon they're by themselves."

"How's that?"

Westfall glanced at Curley and chuckled.

"You ever know Clay Best to figure he needs anyone's help doing anything? Besides, they're trailing a packhorse. If they had any townspeople, Clay would have them trailing the packhorse."

"Makes sense." Curley glanced through the binoculars once more and grinned.

"Well hell, this could solve several problems."

"How's having Clay Best on your trail solve anything?"

"We plug them both and take their horses. Then, we're well mounted with the Mexican border just over yonder, and they ain't following us no more." Curley handed Carlos the binoculars.

"Yeah, it sure sounds easy. But what happens if we don't get 'em both on the first try? They've got good horses and guns, while we're practically on foot. I don't call that good odds," Curley.

"This ain't like you, Jim. You're beginning to act scared of that old marshal. Whoa, I'm on your side," he added as Westfall pull his gun and jammed it against his head.

"I ain't afraid of no one."

"Okay, I know that, Jim. I just wanted to remind you, that's all."

Westfall holstered his gun and glared at the two figures moving in the distance.

"Without good horses, we don't have a back door. I always want a back door, Curley, in case something goes wrong. I ain't never steered you wrong yet, have I?"

"No, I don't reckon you have."

The three men climbed back down the ridge and began saddling the horses.

"So, what do we do now?" Curley asked.

"We'll find some fresh horses. Then, we'll take care of Clay Best and Julio Garcia."

Chapter 12

It was approximately two o'clock in the afternoon when Teresa left Maria's house and paused to cover Yolanda's head with a scarf. She had been babysitting the boys while Maria sat beside Ray at the doctor's residence. The news was good. Sheriff Ray King had awakened in the middle of the night, alert, and wanting to know where he was. Doctor Spencer told Maria that if her husband remained in that condition, and continued to improve, she could take him home tomorrow. The problem would be keeping him quiet while his body healed. Charlie Roberts, on the other hand, had not only gone home the day following the shooting, but Teresa had heard he was back to selling drinks inside his saloon.

"Hola, Señora Best. Buenas tardes."

She turned to see a well-dressed middle-aged gentleman seated on an old buckboard beside an attractive middle-aged woman.

"Perdón, señora, you must not remember me." He climbed from the wagon and removed his sombrero and bowed gracefully.

"Please allow me to introduce myself. Captain Jose Ramos of the fifth regiment *of Los Federales de Mexicanos,* now retired. And this is my lovely wife, Juanita."

" *Buenas tardes.*" Teresa said with a quick curtsey. "I did not recognize you without the uniform. It is good to meet you, *Señora* Ramos. You look as though you have come a long way. You must come to my *jacale* and refresh yourself."

"Gracias, *señora.* That is kind of you. It has been a long journey," Juanita said. She held out her hand for Jose to help her from the wagon. "It will be good to get out of this hard seat, even if it is for a short while."

"*Sí,* I find riding my horse, Diablo, much more comfortable, but I cannot get my husband to understand. Since I had our baby, he treats me like I am somehow crippled. He insists I ride in the buggy or spring wagon." Teresa took her by the arm and began walking toward her home, while Jose followed with the wagon.

Yolanda released a stuttering cry as she stirred and flayed against the scarf. "May I?" Juanita held out her arms.

" *Sí,*" Teresa said as she passed the squalling baby to Juanita. "I'm afraid she needs changing."

"That is quite alright. I've changed hundreds of dirty diapers." She pulled the scarf back to reveal the fussy baby. "My, she is beautiful. What is she called?"

"Her name is Yolanda Elena Maria Rosetta Best, but you can just call her Yolanda, if you wish."

Teresa watched as the woman raised the baby to her face and cooed, talking nonsense in a tiny voice to her daughter. Yolanda responded by ceasing to cry. Teresa turned off the road and walked toward a *jacale* with a prairie schooner parked in the yard. Two women were cooking over an outdoor stove, while two men were making repairs to a small tear in the schooner cover. A large yellow dog rose from the shade of a tree, barked loudly, then trotted to greet Teresa.

"Oh my, it looks as though you have company," Juanita said.

"*Sí*, they are friends of mine. Come, I'll introduce you. They are very nice people." Teresa tugged at her arm as she started toward the house, then paused to look at Jose.

"You may leave the wagon here in the yard and take your horses to the stable, right over there," she said pointing. "Tell Miguel I sent you. He will take very good care of the animals."

Teresa stopped long enough to say something to a couple of young men helping an older man grease the wheels on the prairie schooner, then continued inside. The older man motioned with his head and the young men hurried to help Jose unhitch the team.

"I'm Rob Mayfield," the older of the two said as he unhooked one of the horses. "This is my wife's brother, Pete. Mrs. Best said we were supposed to help you."

Rob hooked a lead to the horse and handed it to Peter.

"*Gracias, amigos*," Jose said as Antonio patted up, wagging his tail.

Jose reached to pet the dog, but Peter grabbed his arm. "I wouldn't do that, if I were you. He looks friendly, but he's liable to take a hunk outa you real quick."

"Really?" Jose stared at Antonio with a crooked grin. I haven't met many dogs I couldn't pet. What makes you so different, *hombre*?"

"Antonio has been trained to protect Mrs. Best," Rob said, tugging on the lead. The horse had all four hooves planted firmly and refused to budge.

"Ah, so you do your job well, do you? "Jose stood in front of Antonio with his hands on his hips. "That means you are a good soldier. I salute you, then." He gave the dog a snappy salute, then reached into his pocket to retrieve a piece of jerked meat and tossed it to the dog, who swallowed it in one gulp.

"There is your reward for a job well done."

"Come on, girl. There's a nice stall with feed and water waiting for you." Rob continued tugging while the mare stood firm. Peter wasn't doing any better.

"Here, gentlemen, let me try," Jose said. Rob and Peter passed the leads to Jose, who started walking toward the stable, while the team followed like well-trained puppies.

"I am afraid my wife has spoiled these animals horribly. They will only respond to either her or myself."

"That's a good thing, ain't it?" Pete asked.

"How so?"

"I mean, it would be hard for someone to steal a horse that just won't move, wouldn't it?"

"Yes, I suppose you're right," Jose said with a chuckle. "On the other hand, that also means either Juanita or myself must do all the work caring for them."

"Huh, I never thought of it that-a-way," Pete said slowly.

"But, such is life."

Jose guided the team into one of the corrals as Miguel and one of his sons came from the barn and headed their way.

"You, being a married man, must have learned that already." Jose grinned at Rob.

"Yeah, I guess so," Rob said. "I know being married didn't exactly turn out the way I'd planned or thought it would be."

Jose laughed and swatted Rob on the back. "It never does." He handed Miguel two gold coins and the leads to the horses with minimal instructions, then promised to return later to check on them. He placed an arm around both young men as they headed toward Teresa's *jacale*.

"You'll discover you have to take life as it is and make the best of it. Much of what happens comes from outside, from things that you have no control over."

"Like the drought?" Rob asked.

"Exactly," Jose said with a chuckle. "When I retired from the army, we were going to live on the family rancho with my son and his family. The rancho has been in the family for generations. I was going to help Roberto raise corn and goats, while Juanita played with our grandsons. But, the drought changes everything."

They stopped at the front door when a large coverall-clad man met them with a cup of cool water.

"This is my pa," Pete said proudly.

"Jose Ramos," he said, offering a hand shake. "I think you have already met my Juanita."

"Yes, lovely woman," Theodore said, then handed the cup of water to Jose. "I reckon you need this."

"Ah yes, that would be nice right now."

"I think we can find something more substantial at supper."

Chapter 13

Clay chuckled as he passed the binoculars to Julio. "Looks as though Westfall's learned a thing or two. They've got themselves a spyglass, and have been keeping tabs on us."

Julio lay in the sand and braced his elbows against a rock as he adjusted the focus.

"*Sí*, they are on the move again," he said as Westfall and Curley retreated back down the ridge.

"Well, we'll just sit here and see which way they're headed. How 'bout making a pot of coffee? I'll build the fire while you get the pot ready. You make it a whole lot better than I do."

Julio chuckled as he filled the coffee pot from a canteen, while Clay got a fire going. They chewed jerked beef and cold tortillas while they waited for the coffee. Julio had just filled both cups when Clay spied the three men leaving their camp.

"There they go."

"*¿Qué fue eso*," Julio asked, handing Clay his cup.

"They're on the move again." Clay pointed as he watched through the binoculars. He took a sip of coffee and set the cup aside.

"I'll get the horses."

"No, relax and drink your coffee. We've got plenty of time. Here," he passed the binoculars to Julio, "have a look-see. It 'pears Westfall's got himself a lame horse."

"*Sí*, it won't take him far."

"That's what I figure. Relax and enjoy your coffee."

They took their time and drank a second cup before Clay stood and stretched.

"Okay, let's saddle up. What I figure we'll do is, we'll follow that wash over yonder, and keep out of sight as much as possible. You'll work your way ahead of them, while I come up behind. I want you to open up with your Winchester the minute you hear me causing a ruckus. They've got themselves rifles, so stay back outa range if you can. I don't figure on us getting ourselves killed."

Clay gave the cinch a final tug and grinned.

"I'll take the pack horse while you work yourself ahead of them. Ready?"

"*Sí, Jefe.*"

Clay watched as Julio guided his horse into the wash. James Westfall and his gang were small figures on the eastern horizon. He mounted Diablo and urged the black into the wash behind Julio.

"Headin' toward Cool Water," he mumbled to himself. With Manuel Rosales and Theodore Russell there, Westfall might get himself an unwelcome surprise. Teresa herself would be more than a handful for any man, but Clay figured he and Julio had better settle things before they reached Cool Water. Besides Teresa, there was Estrella and Manuel's wife, not counting Russell's wife and daughter. He didn't like thinking what might happen if they failed and Westfall arrived before they did.

Chapter 14

Teresa studied the clump of men gathered at the creek as she hung the freshly washed laundry. They had arrived in Cool Water the day before, and she quickly asked Pete to build her a washstand. Washing clothes had become a daily chore since the arrival of Yolanda. The finished product consisted of two planks set on top of two rugged sawhorses and a metal washtub on her front porch. She thanked him just the same.

She hung one diaper and stared at the men. It wasn't that she had never seen a bunch of men talking before. Her first husband, Refugio Romero, had been a member of Burnell's gang, and she herself had ridden with them a time or two, but didn't like any of it. The evenings were filled with men laughing, drinking and fornicating with the women they brought to camp. It was only the fact that she was Refugio's woman that had saved her from that sort of thing.

What piqued her curiosity was the way Theodore Russell and Rob were talking and pointing. Every man in Cool Water was gathered, as if they were seeing something in the bed of the creek. She was sure if Jose Ramos had made the trip instead of staying in Carrizo Springs so his wife could rest, he would have been there also. She could see the creek from where she was standing, and whatever they were seeing was invisible to her. She hung last piece of clothing and walked briskly toward the men.

"*¿Qué es, amigos*, what is so interesting?"

"Oh, I was just explaining to Manuel that you folks are wasting a lot of good water," Theodore said.

Teresa stared at the creek bed for a minute and shrugged. "All I see is a trickle of water that keeps going until it dries up in the desert."

"That's just the point, ma'am. See, look here," he said, pointing. "The creek bed widens out just beyond that boulder, then narrows about a hundred yards further down. I got me a suspicion this creek gives a lot of water on a normal year."

"That's what Clay says, but I've never see it," she said with a shrug.

"That might be fine on wet years," Theodore continued. "But, if I owned this place, I'd build me a dam just where the creek narrows at the far end. Then, all that water just going to waste would make a fair-sized pond. On dry years, like this one, you could be using that water for the cattle, maybe irrigate a garden or even do a little farming. I'd also drill a deep well and install a windmill to supply the houses, so folks wouldn't be having to drink from the same creek cattle and horses are drinking in." He paused and gazed off in the distance. "That's what I'd do, if I was you folks."

"*Bueno,*" she said with a firm nod. "Manuel, do you think you could build a dam like *Señor* Russell is talking about?"

"Maybe, with some help. I've never built one, but *sí,* I could try."

"I could teach him, ma'am," Theodore said with a chuckle. "That is, until your husband gets back. Hildegarde and me don't plan on going off and leaving Manuel to look after you and these other women by hisself. Besides, we've been eating your food and living off your hospitality. It'll give me and the boys something to do and feel useful."

"I hardly need *looking out for, Señor* Russell, but I accept your offer. *Gracias.*"

******

"You bring it under one arm, like this," Teresa pulled the large bandana under Clara's left arm, "then tie it like this," and tied it in a bow above her right shoulder. "Now, you can place your son inside like I have Yolanda, and have both hands free."

"Thank you," Clara said, slipping William into the sling.

"*No molestar,*" Teresa said with a smile. "That's what women are supposed to do. Help each other."

Clara watched through the window as Teresa went outside and grabbed the basket of freshly-washed diapers to hang them on the rope stretched across the post on the front porch. She couldn't explain why she didn't like the woman. Teresa had never done anything but treat her with kindness and respect. Still, she burned inside every time she was around Teresa, especially when Teresa and Rob were talking. She glanced toward the creek, but couldn't see the men building the dam. Her mother had taken them a bucket of water, a bar of lye soap, and a towel for the men to wash for dinner.

Clara's attention was drawn back to Teresa. The woman had just given birth, yet her slender waist and lean body looked as though she had never been pregnant. It had taken Clara several months to lose her belly. It wasn't fair. No wonder Rob found her interesting. Clara had studied herself in the mirror inside the covered wagon many times since arriving in Cool Water, and she wasn't fat by any means. She had always been the total opposite. She was skinny as a rail. It was true her breasts had grown a little while breast-feeding William, but compared to Teresa's, her breasts were hardly noticeable.

She jerked the curtains closed and turned away from the window. Grabbing a bottle of wine, she placed it inside a basket with several small mugs. The cabin was much too small for everyone to eat at the same time, so they had been taking their meals inside the saloon. She had just opened the door when Estrella squealed loudly. Clara dropped the basket, breaking its contents, when she saw her mother running toward her. Behind her was a band of a dozen or more Yaqui Indians.

"Oh God! Oh God!" Clara cried as she bolted back inside. Franticly searching for something to fight with, she grabbed the shotgun from the rack above the door and peered through the opening, then froze. Estrella was running to meet the band of Yaqui, while Teresa stopped Hildegarde in her flight toward the cabin and said something Clara could not hear. Then both women turned and followed Estrella toward the Indians. Clara stared at the basket as a trickle of red wine made a path across the porch and into the dirt. She sat on the edge of the porch and burst into tears.

******

"*¿Qué es, señora?* Are you still upset about breaking the bottle of wine?" Teresa sat beside Clara and draped an arm around her shoulders. Clara shrugged the arm away and crossed the room to stare out the dusty saloon window.

"That's one of the things," she said quietly. "Now, the men won't have anything to drink with supper."

"*Señora,*" Teresa said with a chuckle, "there is plenty of water. Besides, we are inside a *cantina*. I'm sure the men can find something to drink."

"I didn't know those Indians were friends of yours."

55

"I didn't either, until I saw Estrella. Then I remembered her telling me about her family. I don't believe they knew she was here, and were surprised to see her."

They turned as Estrella and Hildegarde entered to set several pots of food on the bar. They were quickly followed by Rebecca Santiago carrying a plate of tortillas.

"What happened to them? Why are they here?"

"They were run out of their home by Apaches, and had no place to go. One of them had passed through Cool Water long ago and remembered there was water. So, they came," she said with a shrug.

"You invited them to stay, didn't you?" Clara glared at her.

"And what would you have me do, *señora joven*?"

Clara glared all the harder. "I don't like being called names. Especially when I don't know what they mean."

Hildegarde took a pitcher of water from Rob and stopped to stare at the proceedings.

"I called you a young lady, since that is what you are acting like, a very young girl. Look," she added after a moment of silent glaring. "Those people need our help. They have nothing to eat. One of them was wounded by an Apache arrow and his wound is infected. I will help them the same way I would help any stranger, because that is what *Jesús Cristo* would have me to do."

"But they're Indians."

"*Sí*, and Jesus was a Jew. He wasn't white or brown, *señora*. And I don't think he cares about this kind of talk. I will help those people. You don't have to help if you don't want, but I will help them."

"Here we are," Theodore said as he and Leo came from the back room holding a bottle of brandy.

"We found some bottles of wine also," Leo added.

"What's going on?" Theodore asked as he studied the glaring women.

"It seems our daughter has taken offence because Mrs. Best agreed to help those homeless Indians."

"How do we know we can trust them, Pa? They might slit our throats in the middle of the night and take everything we've got."

"Good God!" Theodore said with a belly-laugh. "Is that what this is all about?"

"Well, it ain't funny," Clara yelled, causing her son to start crying.

"Maybe not, but slitting our throats is highly unlikely. Correct me if I'm wrong, Leo, but from what I hear, Yaquis are pretty good farmers. They're hell on the battlefield, once you back them into a corner, but they just want to be left alone and farm their patch of ground."

"*Sí*, that is true," Leo said with a nod. "I've never had any trouble with Yaqui."

"That's what I thought. Mrs. Best would do good to hang onto that bunch camped by the creek." He pulled the cork on a bottle of brandy and poured some into a mug. "Now, let's eat. I'm starving."

******

Rob Mayfield slipped the suspenders off his shoulders and sat on the edge of the cot to remove his boots. Clara was already dressed in her nightgown and in bed. She had finished feeding William and the baby was sleeping on his own pallet a next to her.

"Are you mad at me?" Clara asked.

"What makes you ask that?"

"You've been awful quiet, that's why. What are you mad about?"

"I ain't mad as much as disappointed," he said, tossing the boots into the corner. They were sleeping in one of the back rooms of the saloon that had been used by one of Lester's working girls. He had failed to mention that fact to

Clara when Teresa offered them the room. He figured it was safer that way, if he wanted to sleep in an actual bed. Clara wouldn't have had any part of the room had she known.

"Disappointed 'bout what? That I don't wanna have my throat cut by a bunch of savages?"

"That ain't likely to happen."

"And how would you know?"

Rob chuckled and shook his head. "Do you think Mrs. Best would let them camp by the creek if she thought they were dangerous?"

"You act like she's some kind of goddess or something," Clara snapped. "I doubt that she knows near as much as you let on."

Rob studied her for a few seconds before removing his trousers.

"So, that's what this is all about, isn't it? You're jealous because I'm friends with Mrs. Best."

"Oh, no. You're much more than friends with her. Just how well do you know her? Hmmm?" Clara glared at him.

Rob snorted as he unbuttoned his shirt.

"Nothing like you think, that's for sure."

He tossed the shirt into a pile with his trousers.

"And if I was to go cheating with another woman, it certainly wouldn't be with Clay Best's wife. I'd sooner point a gun at my head and blow my own brains out. Look," he added, sitting on the edge of the cot. "I love you more'n anything, and I'm not going to mess our marriage up by cavorting with another woman. I'm nothing like my brother, Clara Jean. If this is going to be a problem, I'll ask your pa to load the wagon and head toward California tomorrow."

"Promise?" She latched onto his arm and stared at him through misty eyes.

"Promise." He pinned her to the pillow with a kiss. "Now, reckon we can make love without waking our son?"

"Blow out the lamp and find out."

Chapter 15

James Westfall dismounted to study the horse's hoof, then cursed loudly.

"Reckon he's done for. Nothing to do but double up with y'all 'til we can find fresh horses. That'll mean Clay and Julio will be on top of us for sure."

He wiped his brow and pulled his .45, cocking the hammer.

"Hold on, *Jefe,*" Carlos said as James pointed the pistol toward the horse's head.

"What for?"

"I've been this way before. I think there's a small farm with horses not far away. Let me see."

"Don't take too long," James yelled, as Carlos turned his horse. "Won't be too long before they're breathing down our necks."

******

Julio guided his horse into a wash and followed the sandy bottom at a brisk trot for several miles before discovering it opened into a boxed canyon with steep sides. Uttering a mild curse, he turned back the way he had come.

He had gone approximately a mile and a half before spying Clay heading toward him trailing the pack horse.

"*¿Qué es, Jefe?*"

"The wash I was following turned into a dead end. I reckon this one ain't much better, or you wouldn't be heading back."

"No," Julio said shaking his head. "What do we do now?"

"We do what we should've done in the first place. Quit trying to sneak up on them, and meet 'em face to face."

"*Bueno.*" Julio smiled and checked the loads in his gun.

******

Carlos returned after fifteen minutes and surveyed the horizon before entering the shallow wash sheltering James and Curley.

"The *peon's* farm is a mile to the south. We had better hurry. The big man and his friend, they come from the west now."

James and Curley mounted and guided the horses out of the wash.

"They got any horses?"

"*Sí,*" Carlos said, taking the lead. "They sometimes keep horses for the Federales. I think they have some now."

"Well, that's fine and dandy," James said with a chuckle. "Just so's they ain't got any Federales."

James nodded with pleasure as the small farm came into sight. It consisted of approximately fifty acres sitting on the bank of the Rio Grande. A corral containing ten strong-looking horses sat to one side next to an adobe tack house. A larger adobe dwelling sat twenty yards away with a couple of children playing out front.

James urged the ailing horse ahead, dismounting and walking the last fifty yards. A Mexican peon came from the main house and walked toward them, as a large black man appeared in the tack house doorway.

"Tell him we need to swap these animals for fresh horses," James said as Carlos dismounted.

He waited as Carlos repeated the demand in Spanish, then snickered as the old man shook his head and rejected the order.

"He says the horses are not for sale. They are for the Mexican Federales."

"Well, tell him I wasn't offering to buy them. I plan on taking what we need, and leaving these nags in their place."

Carlos repeated the demand and received the same result.

"He says he can't let you have them. The Federales will want good horses when they come."

"Well, now. That's just too bad. See," James said, pointing toward the river, "that river is the border. Now, this ranch is sitting on the Texas side, and the Federales aren't supposed to be crossing over onto this side. So," he paused to remove his hat and wipe his brow on his sleeve. He replaced the hat and rested his hand on his pistol. "I reckon I'll just have to take 'em anyway."

He drew the gun and shot the old man in the chest. The small boy and girl both screamed and bolted inside the adobe as the black man disappeared inside the tack and popped back out holding a shotgun. Curley shot him before he could shoulder the weapon.

A woman screamed and charged from the dwelling with a butcher knife and James shot her in the head.

"Swap our gear while I see if they've got anything useful inside the 'dobe," James said, handing Carlos his reins.

"Well, well. Look what we've got here," Curley said and he peered through the doorway. James looked over Curley's shoulder to see the children huddled next to a girl crouched in a corner. James guessed she might've been eleven or twelve years old, from the looks of her.

"Huh, we ain't got time for that right now. Take a look around and see if they ain't got some portable vittles. I'm sure Clay and Julio must've heard them shots, and they'll be on us in a hurry."

"Why don't we just wait right here and finish it?" Curley said.

"Now, that wouldn't be too smart, would it? James said.

"How do you mean, it ain't too smart. I'm tired of running."

"I am too. But you can stay right here, inside this adobe with them kids, while Clay and Julio pick this place apart with their rifles. Me? I'd rather be out there in the open with fresh mounts. I'd stand a better chance."

******

"*¿Qué fue eso?*" Julio reigned his horse to a stop and glanced toward Clay.

"Sounds like they've stirred up a hornet's nest." Clay urged his horse forward. "Let's go have a look-see."

Clay set the pace at a ground-eating lope, then slowed as the farm came into view, then stopped.

"What do you think, *Jefe?* We go down there?"

"Yeah, we'll go, but let's make sure we're not riding into some trap."

Clay dug around inside his saddlebag and retrieved his binoculars. He took his time surveying the farm, then cursed under his breath.

¿Qué es, Jefe?

"I think we're too late."

He passed the binoculars to Julio.

"Take a look at the animals inside the corral. Ain't that bay the one Westfall was riding?"

Julio took his time studying the corral before passing the binoculars back to Clay with a nod.

"*Sí*, it has a sore foot and limps."

Clay viewed the horizon through the binoculars before cursing again.

"There they go," he pointed toward a draw to the south. "They're moving toward the Rio Grande."

"They go to Mexico. We going after them?"

"I'd love to do just that." He nudged his horse in the flanks and walked slowly toward the adobe house. Seeing the bodies lying in the yard, Clay pulled his pistol and cocked the hammer.

"*Santa Maria, Madre de Dios*," Julio said as he crossed his breast. "There's no need to kill them, *Jefe*. They don't have a gun. They cannot fight."

"Yeah, but Westfall don't quite see it that-a-way. He figures if they're breathing air, they're fair game."

"Hold it right there."

Clay froze at the deep command coming from the tack house.

"Same goes for you too, the both of you. Drop the guns and get down off them horses. I don't wanna kill you, but I shore will, if I have to."

Clay lowered the hammer on his .45 and tossed it gently in the dust. He dismounted slowly, keeping one hand raised.

"No need in killing us, mister. We're chasing them that done this. Looks like we're a might late. How'd it come down?"

The man rose from behind a small stack of hay holding a twelve gauge in his right hand. The left shoulder and chest was covered in blood.

"You're bleeding something fierce, boy. Better come to the house and let us see what we can do."

Clay started to pick up his gun, but stopped as the man cocked the hammers on the shotgun.

"Ain't no need for that, boy. We really are on your side. My name's Clay Best, and this here feller is Julio Garcia. See, take a look." He ended by pulling back the duster to reveal the badge pinned to his shirt.

"That's good to know." He lowered the hammers on the shotgun and plopped to sit in the dirt. "I didn't have the heart to shoot you no how. My name's Joe…Joseph Lincoln."

"Got anymore staying here?

"Two children and a young orphan girl. They're inside the house. I didn't hear no more shots, so they may be okay."

"Well, Joseph Lincoln, let's get you inside and see if we can save you from bleeding to death."

******

The young Mexican girl met them at the door holding a meat cleaver, while two small children clung to her skirts crying.

"Better tell her we're here to help, Julio. I don't plan on getting myself cut to pieces, and don't figure on killing her neither."

Clay waited until Julio and Joseph convinced her they were safe and she had put the cleaver on the table. Julio helped Clay remove Joseph's shirt and began bathing the wound with water. The young girl ran to the pump to fetch more water and Clay motioned toward the door with his head as he packed some dried herbs from Teresa's medical pack.

"What's her story?"

"Her name is Isabel Acuna. She's an orphan the Diegos took in," Joseph said.

"That the name of the man and woman lying outside?"

"Yeah," Joseph said with a grimace as Clay applied pressure to the wound. "Pedro and Leticia Diego. Those young'uns, Silvia and Alejandro, belong to them. Now, I reckon they's orphans too." He shook his head and cursed. "They were good folks. There weren't no need in killin' them. They coulda just taken the horses. We couldn't have stopped them.

"Maybe, but that ain't Westfall's way of doing things. He sort of gets a thrill out of killin' folks and seeing them suffer. I'm surprised he ain't doubled back and tried for us."

"Westfall. There were three of them. Which one is he?"

"Wrap that real tight," Clay said to Julio. "Joe's going to have to fork a horse one way or the other, and no sense in him bleeding to death before we get to where we're going."

"We got him and three children, *Jefe*. Where we going?"

"Depends on where the nearest town is. Joe needs a doctor, and them young'uns need looking after."

"There's a Mexican fort about thirty miles southwest from here," Said Joseph. "It's on the Mexican side of the river. Those horses them murderin' bastards took belonged to them. We took care of them, so when the Federales were anywhere close and needed fresh mounts, we had 'em ready."

"The ranch is closer, *Jefe*," Julio said. "It is only eight – maybe ten miles over there." He pointed toward the east.

Clay nodded. "Yeah, it might be our best bet. It'd be easier on our friend here, and with them young'uns, we ain't gonna make much of a stand if Westfall and Curley decide to come after us."

Julio finished tying the bandage and Clay poured water into a pan to wash his hands.

"To answer your question, the tall one with stringy blond hair is James Westfall. His two friends are Curley Hammond and Carlos Mendoza. Westfall considers himself a real hand with the ladies as well as his gun. Any one of them wouldn't think twice about boring a hole in your head. I'm surprised he left you and them young'uns alive."

"I blacked out when they shot me, so they may have thought I was dead. I don't know about Isabel and the others," Joe said.

"She said they were in a hurry and wanted to get away before we came," Julio said as he dried his hands. "What are we going to do? Spend the night here and go to the rancho in the morning?"

"That might be best," Clay said thoughtfully. "We'll take turns keeping watch. They might make a try after dark."

Chapter 16

Jose Ramos allowed the team to set their own pace as the wagon creaked and groaned toward Cool Water. Juanita gripped the edge of the plank seat with white knuckles as they jolted past a deep rut.

"Sorry, my dear. I did not see that one coming," he said with a chuckle.

"Maybe not, but I keep having visions of falling out and being run over by the rear wheel."

"Oh, I would hate to think of that happening," he said with a grin. "I will have to go slower."

He pulled back on the reins, bringing the horses to a slow walk. Jose had tried renting a buggy for the trip, but Miguel only had one for rent at the stable in Carrizo Springs, and it had a broken wheel.

"I'm sorry, Captain Ramos, but they are backed up at the blacksmith's shop. The wheel has been there for three weeks. I will check on it this afternoon, but...." Miguel shrugged, "I don't think it will be done."

"That's okay, my friend," Jose said patting him on the shoulder. "It's not your fault."

And Jose figured it really wasn't anyone's fault. Roy Johnson had all but abandoned the blacksmith shop once he took over Ray King's job as sheriff after Ray had been shot. Jose had only been in town a few days, but he failed to see the need for a full-time lawman, since Carrizo Springs more or less ran itself. The citizens were hard-working men and women trying to scrape out a living in a drought-plagued hunk of desert. Outside of locking up the occasional drunk, or breaking up a Saturday night fist-fight at the cantina, there wasn't much to do. He believed Roy Johnson simply loved being sheriff, and who could blame him? Patrolling the streets and shaking hands was not as heavy work as (and certainly cooler than) standing over a charcoal fire and pounding a sledge hammer.

Jose had thought they might visit Cool Water once Clay returned from chasing the men who had shot Ray and the owner of the cantina. But Clay had not returned, and Jose had to make the ten mile journey anyway. Juanita had insisted, since California was too far away from their children and grandchildren. Jose didn't argue, since he felt the same way. Today's trip was to see if they knew of a small piece of land he could buy with enough water to raise a few head of beef and survive until the drought ended. When that day came, they could move back to his son's rancho.

"Look," Juanita said as she pointed. Jose turned his head to see a line of warriors on a rocky ridge toward the east. "Is that Indians?"

Jose gripped the reins tightly as the small Apache war party began to string out and move their way.

"Hold on tight," he said and slapped the reins. "They are Apaches, and they're coming our way. Ya! La prisa!" he slapped the reins and yelled.

Juanita gripped the seat tightly as the wagon bolted forward. Her heart pounded in her chest as the dust from the team engulfed them. She was beginning to think the wagon might shake itself to pieces as a small clump of buildings appeared ahead.

"Hold on," Jose yelled as he guided the wagon toward a creek bed without slowing down. The whoops and yells from the warriors grew closer and an arrow whizzed past them, narrowly missing one of the horses.

******

Teresa had just dumped several soiled diapers into her washtub when she heard the noise. She ran to the middle of the dusty road to see Leo Santiago run toward the tack house. She gasped as the vaquero grabbed Rebecca's arm, almost pulling her off her feet.

"*Santa Maria, Madre de Dios*," she said as a wagon and its riders dropped out of sight into the creek bed. A band of whooping Indians followed closely behind. Leo reappeared from the tack house with a rifle to shoot one of the Indians from his horse.

"What's going on?" Clara asked as she appeared on the porch.

"Get back inside," Teresa ordered, giving her a push.

"Hey!"

"*Silencio!*" Teresa yelled. "Indians. Get inside." She grabbed the Winchester from the rack on the wall and injected a shell.

"Indians?" Clara's voice was high and squeaky as she crowded Teresa's shoulder.

"Move!" Teresa pushed. "Get the babies and make sure they're safe."

She poked the barrel through the opened window to see one of the Yaqui children clubbed in the head as he tried running toward Leo and the tack house. Teresa readied the Winchester, then raised the barrel as the wagon pulled to a halt in front of her house. Captain Ramos and Juanita leaped to the ground. Jose opened the door and banged it closed as Juanita dove inside. The frightened horses and wagon disappeared in a cloud of dust as the sound of gunfire and yells filled the air. The warriors charged like swarm of ants.

Teresa aimed once again but pulled up as Hildegarde flashed by the window and burst through the door, slamming it closed behind her. Captain Ramos opened the door a crack and fired his pistol.

"Here," Teresa said, passing the rifle to Hildegarde. "I am much better with the pistol." She pulled one of the pearl-handled pistols from the holster hanging on the wall and fired twice as Hildegarde fired several shots. The noise started both babies crying.

Clara screamed and bolted toward the door. Captain Ramos caught her around the waist and pulled her back.

"It is not safe to go outside, *señora.*"

"Rob! Where is my husband?" Clara clawed at the door. Hildegarde slapped her soundly on the cheek.

"Hush! Get a grip on yourself! Rob's inside the saloon with your father and brother. A bunch of Yaquis are in there also."

Teresa emptied the .38 and slid it across the floor to Clara.

"It's empty. Load it."

Clara stared at her with frightened eyes while Teresa grabbed the second pistol and belt from the wall, then tossed the cartridge belt to Clara, who let the belt hit her in the stomach and fall to the floor.

"Load the damned gun," Hildegarde yelled as she fired the Winchester.

Clara snapped the Smith and Wesson open, dumping the empty cartridges on the floor. Her fingers shook and fumbled, dropping several bullets as she tried loading the pistol. The yells and gunfire increased as gun smoke filled the room and stung her eyes. She snapped the gun closed when the last bullet dropped into the cylinder. She glanced toward the babies who were lying on their pallets by the rear wall and screamed. An Apache warrior was leaning through the open window, lifting Teresa's baby. Without thinking, Clara swung the gun around with both hands and pulled the trigger. The Indian dropped the baby as the bullet ripped through his left cheek and shattered several teeth. The warrior disappeared and she bolted toward the wailing babies and fired twice through the window.

The attack ended as quickly as it had started. Captain Ramos took his time reloading his pistol, then turned toward Clara with a smile.

"My complements, *Señora* Mayfield. You fought like a true Federale." He finished with an elegant bow.

"*¿Qué?*" Teresa had been watching the Indians through the window as they galloped out of town.

"You were busy, *Señora* Best, so you didn't see. But *Señora* Mayfield saved your daughter's life.

"*¿Qué?*" Teresa repeated with wide-eyes.

Clara handed her mother Teresa's gun with trembling hands, then stooped to check on the babies.

"*Sí*, I was loading my pistol when a warrior leaned through the window to take your Yolanda. He already had her in his hands, when *Señora* Mayfield shot him in the face.

Teresa dropped the pistol and darted toward the babies. She held the frightened baby against her breast, whispering a prayer of thanks, then leaned to kiss Clara on the cheek.

"*Gracias, señora. Gracias.* I shall pray for you every day. I cannot pay you enough for saving my child. You are a brave woman."

Clara held her son tightly in her arms and shook her head slowly. "I ain't so brave. All I saw was that man holding one of the babies. I didn't even know whose baby it was, and I didn't aim the gun. I just pulled the trigger." She heaved a sob. "I think I wet myself."

Captain Ramos chuckled as he placed both hands on her shoulders.

"That is a sign of true bravery, *señora*. I have been in many battles, and you can believe that everyone is frightened. I have been frightened many times myself, and

I've seen many soldiers soil themselves when faced with mortality. A true sign of bravery is to be frightened and continue to fight. My complements on your bravery."

******

Theodore's anger was to the boiling point as he sprinted toward Teresa's house. Those inside the saloon had been lucky. The walls were paper-thin and offered little protection. Several bullets had ripped through to lodge in the oak bar. He burst inside Teresa's house with Rob at his heels.

"Y'all okay?"

"Yes we are. How'd you all fair?" Hildegarde said, hugging him.

Rob pushed past to wrap Clara in his arms.

"You're squashing William," Clara gasped.

"I'm just glad you're okay."

"We fared well," Theodore said. The saloon walls didn't stop nothing but a few arrows. One of the Yaquis got winged, and I felt a bullet whizz past my ear, but we gave more'n we took."

"Captain Ramos was just telling Mrs. Best that Clara Jean saved her baby's life," Hildegarde said.

"What?"

"*Sí*, that is true," Jose said. He then proceeded to retell what had taken place inside the house, making it seem bigger and more elaborate than Hildegarde remembered, especially the saving of baby Yolanda.

"Oh, God!" Rob gasped. He then kissed Clara's face several times, then both hands.

"Rob, please...." Clara said.

"Out, come on. All you men," Hildegarde said, shooing the men outside. "Leave these women alone so they can get the babies quiet."

She waited until Rob had been pulled through the door, then leaned to whisper in Clara's ear. "I'll fetch some clean unmentionables while you get washed."

******

The men stood in a clump in the middle of the road watching the war party. The Indians were still mounted and in a clump of their own about a half a mile away, staring back.

"You think they are planning another attack?" Leo asked.

Theodore waited while Rebecca Santiago and two other women ran past toward Teresa's house.

"I reckon. They're having a pow-wow right now, figuring how they're going to go about it. My guess is they're after the horses, especially that big red one of Mrs. Best's."

"Diablo?"

"Yeah," Theodore said with a nod. "Wouldn't you, if you were them?"

"A fine horse like that would be strong medicine for whoever had it."

"Exactly. Which one you figure is the chief?"

"The one with the blue shirt," Leo said.

"That's what I thought. Looks like they're about ready," he added as the braves strung out and began trotting their ponies toward them.

"So, what do we do?" Leo began reloading his rifle.

"We send them the message they ain't welcome here." He walked briskly toward his wagon, climbed inside and returned with a Prussian- made needle gun.

Leo whistled as Theodore fed a .50 caliber round into the chamber.

"In a former life, I did some buffalo hunting in order to buy that farm I just left. I sold most everything else, but I couldn't quite part with this."

He leveled the gun over one of the wagon's wheels.

"Now, let's tell 'em goodbye."

A flame leaped from the long muzzle as the gun roared. The Indian wearing the blue shirt pitched backwards from his horse a second later. Another brave leaped from his horse and threw the mortally-wounded warrior across his mount. The entire war party turned and disappeared from sight.

"I don't reckon they'll be back anytime soon," Theodore said.

Captain Ramos emerged from the saloon with pistol drawn as Teresa came from the house with a gun in one hand and her baby tucked in the other arm.

"You can relax. They've gone."

"Why did you shoot?" Teresa asked.

"Me and Leo was just telling 'em goodbye."

Chapter 17

Julio took the first watch while Clay curled in a corner and covered himself with a saddle blanket. The younger children didn't sleep well, and kept whimpering into the wee hours of the morning. Julio couldn't blame them much. It had to be literal hell for a young child to see their mother and father killed. Isabel seemed to fair better. She at least slept some. He figured that was a good thing, since she could help tend the little ones if Westfall's gang decided to cause them trouble.

Julio tapped Clay on the shoulder around twelve, and he rolled to his feet, rubbing his eyes.

"Anything?"

"No, quiet, *Jefe.*"

"That's good. Get some sleep. We'll pull out at first light."

******

Clay nudged Julio and Joseph Lincoln awake shortly after three o'clock.

"I've got a creepy feeling on the back of my neck that those bastards are going to try something right soon. Joe, you get them young-uns ready while me and Julio get the horses."

"Those babies are gonna need feeding," Joseph said.

"Give 'em what you can, but we can't take time to cook a nice meal. Build a fire to throw them off track and make 'em think we're still here, but don't bother cooking. There's some jerked beef in my saddlebags. With any luck, we should be in Cool Water around noon."

A heavy cloud cover blacked out the moon, allowing them to slip away quietly before daylight. Julio held the boy in front of him while Joseph held the little girl. Isabel rode by herself. Clay studied the blackened horizon toward the southwest as a bolt of distant lightning flashed, followed by the low roll of thunder. He figured he'd be the one to do the fighting if they were attacked. So far, they'd been lucky. He just didn't know how long their luck would hold.

******

Westfall glared at the empty cabin and swore loudly. They had witnessed the column of smoke from the chimney and figured Clay and Julio were inside with the children. He'd failed to notice the mostly empty corral and cursed himself for allowing them to get away. He'd planned to catch Clay and Julio off guard, knowing Clay would be thinking of the children before his own safety.

"Hell," he had joked earlier, "you never know. We just might join them for breakfast. Wonder what they'll be serving?"

"Depends on who's doing the cooking," Curley said. "If it's Clay....you know how he likes flapjacks."

It had been a good plan. Attack at first light. They'd been saddled and ready by four o'clock, and had walked the horses as quietly as possible. He stared at the corral as his blood boiled. He screamed a curse as he pulled his gun and shot the lame horse he had ridden yesterday.

"I'm tired of running. Mount up! We'll run 'em down and kill the sons-of-bitches."

"That's more like it," Curley said. "I reckon they can't be that far ahead. Carlos," he said, tightening his saddle cinches, "you're a better tracker than me. Why don't you take the lead and see which way they went?"

"*Sí, amigo.*" Carlos leaped on his horse and trotted in a circle past the tack house and corral. He stopped and leaned in the saddle, then nudged the dapple forward. Stopping once more, he waved and yelled. "Over here. They go that way."

"Yeah, it's just like I figured. The bastard's heading back to Cool Water."

"Maybe," Curley said with a snicker. "We can make Cool Water hot water for him."

"Got to catch him first."

They fell into a fast trot behind Carlos as the sun rose higher. It took about a half an hour for James to lose patience. He spurred his mount into the lead and cursed Carlos as he passed him.

"You're too damned slow! We know he's heading toward Cool Water. I wanna kill 'em before he gets there."

Chapter 18

"How bad is it?" Teresa stood on her tip toes and peered over Captain Ramos' shoulder. Several of the Yaqui children had located the runaway wagon in a narrow wash with a broken rear wheel.

"I'm afraid it is unusable." Captain Ramos pushed his hat to the back of his head and shrugged. The Indians had gathered at the back and right side of the wagon to lift it onto a boulder in hopes the wheel could be repaired.

"There is no way to fix it?" Teresa asked.

"I'm afraid not. Not without a blacksmith. I might make it back to Carrizo Springs with a couple of broken spokes, but the rim is broken. Without a metal rim to hold it in place, I'm afraid the wheel will simply come apart.

"I still have my buggy," she said cheerfully. "It is inside the tack house. We could take it to Carrizo Springs. Maybe Miguel has a wheel at the stable we can use."

"We could try." Captain Ramos smiled at her. "But I asked to rent a buggy before I brought my wagon yesterday, and he said he's been waiting for the blacksmith to repair a broken wheel for several weeks." He heaved a sigh.

"I'm afraid the blacksmith in Carrizo Springs is still acting sheriff. We are simply stuck until something changes."

"Maybe," Teresa said, turning away. She paused to look at him over her shoulder.

"I need to go into town and buy some things. You and your wife are welcome to come with us and check again."

"*Sí*, I'm sure Juanita would appreciate going very much."

******

Teresa gritted her teeth and smiled as the surrey rocked from side to side as it rolled toward Carrizo Springs. She hated being confined in such a thing, but she knew better than to ride into town straddled on Diablo and have Clay hear about it later. Either way, she knew first-hand how the citizens of Carrizo Springs loved to talk, and her husband would know soon enough if she rode the horse.

"Do you think we'll have time to take a bath before heading back?" Clara asked.

"*Sí*," she said with a nod as Hildegarde guided the surrey around a deep rut. "I suppose you will have time. We will spend the night at my *jacale*, then leave early in the morning. But we won't have to use the public *baños*." I have a brass bathtub."

"You do?"

"*Sí*." Teresa glanced over her shoulder and smiled.

The girl had not ceased talking since the Apache war party had ridden through Cool Water, and the constant chatter was driving her crazy. For some reason, she was treating Teresa as though they were best friends. The sudden change had her scratching her head. The only thing Teresa could think of was her prayers. She had prayed, asking Mother Mary to change the girl's heart and make her more agreeable. Now, she was asking the Holy Mother why she had to make her so talkative. The only real peace she had was at night when Clara and Rob went to bed in the back room of the cantina.

It would have made little difference to her whether Clara warmed up to her or not, except she knew the animosity between them embarrassed Rob and Clara's parents. Coupled with the fact that they were farmers, and she reasoned if Cool Water was going to be a success, they would have to grow much of their own food.

A wave of gratitude swept over her as Carrizo Springs appeared in the distance. "*Gracias, Santa Maria, Madre de Dios,*" Teresa said, crossing her breast.

"We're almost there," Hildegarde said, patting her on the arm. "It will be nice to get out and stretch our legs."

"*Sí.*" Teresa nodded.

"You really don't like riding in this thing, do you?"

Teresa looked at her and Hildegarde laughed.

"Does it show?"

"I'll say, but I don't blame you none. I'd love to be on horseback myself. Although I don't get to do that much anymore. I really miss it."

Teresa nodded thoughtfully. "Then you shall. When we get back to Cool Water, we'll saddle some horses and go riding. Just you and I."

"I'd like to go too," Clara said with a whine.

"You will go, but the first ride is just for your mother."

******

Teresa disrobed and eased her tired body into the hot water. It was finally her turn, and she comforted herself with the fact that she could soak as long as she wanted. Juanita Ramos was holding her baby and singing a soft ballad. Teresa smiled at the crystal clear tones. The woman could have sung on stage, had she wanted. Instead, she had chosen to be Captain Ramos' wife and live in an army post in the middle of the desert. A true sign of love, if there ever was one.

She slid down into the tub, submerging her head. Reaching for the bar of lye soap, she applied a generous amount to her long hair and began massaging her scalp. She didn't particularly like the concoction because it dried her scalp and made her head itch, but she had not found a suitable replacement in Carrizo Springs. Maybe someday. She worked her fingers vigorously, then submerged her head once again. She finished her hair by dipping fresh water from a bucket and pouring it over her head several times. With that task done, she lay back against the tub and closed her eyes, and didn't open them until the water began to chill her.

The wet plank flooring felt cold and slimy against her bare feet. She quickly pulled the plug, allowing the water to escape through the planking and through the reed walls. Teresa quickly toweled off and wrapped herself in her night gown. Wrapping her damp hair in the towel, she gathered her dirty clothes and opened the door.

Antonio looked at his mistress and yawned.

"Yes, you're a good dog ... keeping watch and making me safe." She squatted to kiss the huge animal on the snout.

Antonio yawned once more and licked Teresa's hand before following her into the house, where he promptly lay beside her bed. The house was dark quiet. She studied the sleeping baby in her bed and said a silent prayer. Yolanda Elena was the greatest blessing ever, perhaps second only to her marriage to Clay.

"*No,*" she thought. The two had to be equal. The baby had changed Clay for the better, if that was possible. But the birth of Yolanda had made such a difference in their lives, Teresa found herself asking the Holy Mother for more children.

After brushing the tangles from her hair, she snuggled down beside her daughter and closed her eyes. Yolanda's crying woke her at dawn.

Chapter 19

The tingling on the back of Clay's neck began to worry him. He turned Loco and nudged him in the opposite direction.

"Where's he going?" Joseph asked.

"Checking our back trail," Julio said. "Better keep moving. He's giving us a chance to make it to Cool Water."

"There was three of 'em. Don't you reckon we'd better give him a hand?"

Julio chuckled. "Three isn't enough to bring *Señor* Clay down. Besides, he'd be angry if we stopped."

"I reckon we'd best be moving then." Joseph held the little girl tightly and kicked the horse in the flanks.

Clay had ridden only a quarter of a mile before a bullet bounced off a rock with a whine. It was quickly followed by several others. Clay slid to the ground and pulled the Winchester from the scabbard as a few scattered rain drops fell. Making sure Loco was hidden behind a large mesquite, he dashed to a vantage point twenty yards away and slid down a bank into a shallow wash. Climbing the opposite bank, he could see the three of them, with James Westfall in the lead.

"Well, well. Thank you God for giving me a nice present.

Clay injected a shell into the chamber and took his time aiming. James jerked the reins roughly, guiding his horse around a clump of cactus the same instant Clay pulled the trigger. A plume of dust shot into the air with a whine where James had been a second earlier.

"Dammit!" He injected another round and aimed as the three bandits dismounted and scrambled for cover.

James fired his pistol with the bullet falling short of its target. Clay returned fire with much better results.

"Pretty stupid, Jim," Clay said with a snicker. "Only you'd forget to grab your rifle." He fired again, kicking rock and dust dangerously close to James.

Clay ducked as a rifle-shot bounced close with a whine.

"Don't guess your Mexican friend is as stupid as you." He returned the favor, causing Carlos to duck as the scattered raindrops turned into a steady sprinkle. A flash of lightning and a loud clap of thunder caused the black stud James had been riding to bolt. Clay chuckled as Westfall cursed loudly and ran after the fleeing animal. Clay fired once more, kicking up dirt inches in front of him. Westfall dove to the ground cursing, then crawled behind a rock where he gave Clay an obscene gesture. Clay fired again, nearly hitting the extended hand.

Carlos fired several more shots at Clay, then the sky seemed to open as the rain came in torrents. Clay glanced up and down the wash, knowing he was in a dangerous position. He'd seen cattle, and on one occasion a cowhand, killed by a flash flood that swept through a wash. Picking a spot near a boulder, he scrambled up the bank on all fours as Carlos fired several more shots. Clay slid behind the boulder as a .44 round bounced near him.

"Okay, let's return the favor." He sent three shots rapid-fire at Carlos as Westfall ran hunched-over after his horse. Another clap of thunder and rain so thick it was difficult to see gave Clay a chance to scamper toward Loco. The horse was right where he had left him. He snorted and bobbed his head up and down.

"Yeah, I know it's pretty stupid being out here in the rain. Let's go find a dryer place. You're a hell of a lot better horse than them nags on the other side of the wash, aren't you? I'll see if we can't rustle up some oats when we reach Cool Water."

It took him about a half an hour to catch up with Julio and the others.

"We heard the shootin'," Joseph said. "Get any of 'em?"

"Na, just a lot of strutting on both sides. This rain kinda hindered things."

"Too bad. I'd like to see all three of them barking in hell before this is over."

"Knowing Westfall, you may get your wish. He figures he owes me for the trouble I've given him. He'll pop up sooner or later and you can open his head," Clay said with a snicker.

Julio had wrapped Pedro and Leticia Diego in blankets that were now soggy. Clay dug in his pack and tossed Joseph his rain slicker.

"Don't suppose you thought to bring one?" He asked Julio, and received a shrug. "Here," he pulled a dry saddle blanket from his roll and gave it to the Vaquero. "The rain's let up some, I reckon it'll have to do."

He glanced at Isabel and shrugged. "Sorry I ain't got one for you." He froze with one foot in the stirrup. as the girl answered in English.

"Thank you, but I'll be okay."

"Well now," Joseph said with a chuckle. "That's the first time I've heard you speak English. I thought you didn't know how."

"There wasn't any need to, until today."

"Well," Clay said as he climbed into the saddle. "We can sort this all out when we get to Cool Water. Right now, I think we'd best be moving before Westfall and his bunch catch their horses. They might decide to come looking for us."

******

It was midafternoon when they finally reached the outskirts of Cool Water.

"What in the hell?" Clay stopped Loco and stared.

"What's wrong?" Joseph asked.

"There's all those people," Julio said, pushing his sombrero to the back of his head. "Where did they come from, *Jefe*?"

"Beats me." Clay recognized Teresa as she came onto the porch carrying their baby. "Let's go find out."

Clay nudged Loco into a trot.

"Ain't them Indians over yonder?" Joseph pointed toward the pond just beyond the stable.

"Yeah," Clay said with a nod. "Yaqui, if I'm not mistaken. In-laws of yours, Julio?"

"*Sí*, Estrella's family. Where did the water come from, *Jefe*?"

"I reckon you'll have to ask them, 'cause I shore don't know."

Teresa saw them and let out a high-pitched squeal as she ran toward them. Clay dropped to the ground and scooped her in his arms, raining kisses on her lips and face.

"I reckon them two were missing each other," Joseph said as he dismounted. Holding Silvia in one arm, he led the horse toward the crowd that was starting to form in the middle of town.

"*Sí*, I wish someone was here to miss us," Isabel said quietly.

Joseph grinned as he noticed a teenage boy staring at the girl as they passed. "My guess is that'll happen sooner than you think."

"¿Qué?" Isabel stared up at him with large brown eyes.

"You happen to be a mighty pretty young woman, and it's my guess that boys like that one over yonder are starting to notice you."

Isabel glanced over her shoulder to see Peter Russell staring at her open-mouthed.

"He is staring because we are so dirty and our clothes are old and wore out."

"That might have something to do with it, but I think it's a bit more than that."

Another squeal caused her to flinch as a young Indian girl flew past to leap into Julio's arms. The vaquero scooped her off the ground and swung her in a circle. Several Yaquis took their horses toward the stable and they were instantly ushered inside the cantina, where plates of hot-spicy food were placed before them.

Clay stood to one side smiling as Silvia and Alejandro Diego shoveled spoons full of rice into their mouths. Isabel asked them to wait until they had given thanks, and all three bowed their heads in prayer.

"I'm a Methodist, but that was a real nice prayer," Hildegarde said as she set mugs of milk before the hungry children. "I'm sure God must've been pleased."

Isabel looked at her, then lowered her eyes to her plate. "*Gracias. Señora* Diego taught us to pray before she died."

"Oh, I'm sorry to hear that." Hildegarde sat down beside the girl. "Was she your mother?"

"No," Isabel shook her head, "she was the woman who took care of me. *Señora* Diego was Alexandro and Silvia's mother. My mother and father died, so I came to live with them."

Hildegarde looked up at Clay and he grinned. It's a long story. You can get the full lowdown from Joseph

Lincoln. But we need to see if we can't get him patched up first."

"Gunshot?" Theodore asked.

"Yeah, Westfall and his bunch. They bored a hole in Joseph and killed those young'uns' folks. I ain't checked his wound since last night."

"I'll take a look at it," Hildegarde said, scooting her chair back from the table.

"The question is, did you catch them?"

Clay turned to see Jose Ramos lighting a cigar. "Captain Ramos. How in the hell did you wind up here?"

"Actually, we came to see you," Jose said, slipping an arm around Juanita's shoulder. "But with that type of greeting, I'm not sure we made the right choice."

"Aw, it ain't that. I'm always happy to see you. It's just that you're the last person I expected to see in Cool Water. I figured you to be living high in Mexico City."

Jose and Juanita both laughed at the idea.

"No, they would not invite an outpost captain into their circle, any more than Juanita and I would like being there."

"The lack of rain made it impossible to live on the tiny farm with our son and grandchildren," Juanita said. "Everything around Juarez is dry and dead. Jose wanted to move to California, but I insist that we try to find someplace closer to our children."

"Yeah, I reckon California's a far piece from Juarez. It ain't exactly close to Carrizo Springs, either," Clay said with a chuckle.

"No, but we can be there in two days," Jose said.

"Well, what are you looking for?"

"Mmmm," Jose shrugged. "A small piece of land with a *casa*. I hope to raise a few cattle and have a large garden."

"I might know of a place, if it ain't sold already." Clay accepted a mug of wine that Hildegarde gave him and took a drink. "Lordy, that's good. Been waiting for that for a couple of days." He took another sip.

"Anyways, I should head into Carrizo Springs tomorrow and let 'em know the skunks are still on the loose. We can check at the bank and find out if it's still for sale."

"I'd appreciate it," Jose said, giving Clay a pat on the shoulder. "Let's hope there's still a little food left when they get finished."

Clay chuckled. "Don't matter to me none. I plan on drinking most of my supper." He grabbed the wine bottle and paused as Hildegarde poured more milk for the children.

"Mind telling me where y'all got the milk?"

"From our milk cow, Mr. Best," Hildegarde said with a grin. "Where'd you expect it came from?"

"Well, I know where milk comes from. I sort of forgot about your cow, and figured you must've figured a way to milk one of them critters running wild out there."

******

Clay soaked the dirt and sore muscles away in a hot tub of water. Several mugs of wine washed down with a brandy had relaxed him down to his bones. He had heard all about the Apache raid and thanked God that Theodore and Captain Ramos had been there. He knew Leo and Teresa were more than competent with a gun, but he had no idea how the rest were. According to Captain Ramos, Clara Jean was quite the gun hand, and had saved his daughter's life. He hugged and thanked her properly, but he also knew how tales of heroics grew rapidly, and the real truth lay somewhere between the deed itself and the telling.

He slipped into a clean pare of long johns and crept into the darkened house. Teresa had wisely left a single candle burning; otherwise he might have stepped on Silvia, who had gone to sleep on a pallet next to the bed. Isabel was asleep on the floor against the opposite wall next to Yolanda.

Stepping over Silvia, Clay slid into the bed to find Alejandro snuggled up to Teresa's side, fast asleep.

"Dang!" he said in a hoarse whisper. "I was hopin' to get reacquainted with my wife."

"I know," Teresa whispered. "But these children are hurting and needed comforting."

"I reckon they do at that, but when do we get to spend time alone together?"

"My dear husband," she said with a giggle. "We have created a child. We will never be alone. At least for some years to come."

"I never thought about it that way, but I suppose you're right."

Clay tucked his arms beneath his head and stared at the ceiling. A full moon cast a soft glow through the open window.

"Do you know what Isabel called me today?"

"What did Isabel call you?"

"She called me *Doña* Teresa. Not once, but every time we spoke."

"Huh, never thought 'bout it, but we do own a sizable piece of land, so I reckon in a way, that's exactly what you are."

"*Sí*, and do you know what that makes you?"

"What does it make me?"

"It makes you *Don* Clay. It means all these people, the land and the cattle are our responsibility. We have to take care of them."

Clay stared at the ceiling for what Teresa thought was an eternity. She was beginning to think he had fallen asleep when he said, "Well ... it isn't what I really bargained for, but I reckon you might be right."

He raised himself on one elbow to stare at her. Then leaning across Alejandro, he kissed her lips. The boy squirmed underneath him and Teresa pushed him away.

"Stop it! You'll wake him."

"Alright, but when we get to town tomorrow, I'm renting a hotel room for the afternoon for just you and me."

"Why do that? I own the *jacale*. We can sleep there."

"I don't plan on us sleeping. I plan on us getting reacquainted."

Teresa covered her mouth as she giggled.

"*Sí*, we can do that. Now, hush before we wake *el niño*."

"Alright, I'm tired anyway. Just you remember what I said."

"*Sí*, my *marido muy fuerte*."

Clay rolled onto his side and looked across the tiny room. It felt much larger when it was only him and June living there. That seemed a lifetime ago. He loved Teresa more than steak and potatoes and a pitcher of cold beer. But with all the children and folks sleeping God only knew where, he was feeling a little smothered. He stifled a laugh as Isabel rose on one elbow to cast a smile at him. She lay back, covering her mouth as her body shook with laughter.

You little snot. You're gonna be the one looking after them young'uns while me and Teresa get acquainted.

Chapter 20

"Yer joshin'," Clay stared at Doctor Spencer, opened mouthed.

"No, I'm not joshing." Doctor Spencer glared at him.

"But that's four weeks from now."

"Yes, and your wife needs to heal before you have intercourse with her. It's only been two weeks since she gave birth. She should've been home resting this past week instead of running off God only knows where."

Clay heaved a deep sigh. "Yeah, I know, Doc. I tried telling her, but she don't listen to me much."

"Most women don't listen to their husbands," Doctor Spencer said with a chuckle. "It isn't the end of the world, Mr. Best. You can wait. Be patient."

"I suppose I can wait, Doc, and I've got the patience of Job." He cocked his head and chuckled. "I ain't sayin' I like it."

Doctor Spencer laughed as Teresa came from the examination room, straightening her dress.

"I do so listen to him, *Señor* Spencer. I just don't agree some of the time." She patted Clay on the chest and gave him a peck on the lips.

"Well, I guess I'd better mosey over to see Dave King and let him know I failed to catch the skunks that shot him and Charlie. How are they doing, by the way?"

"Charlie's just fine. It's hard to tell he's ever been wounded." Doctor Spencer sat behind a small desk and began writing in a ledger. "Sheriff King, on the other hand is a different story. He should recover fully, but he's in for a long, difficult rehabilitation."

He tore a slip of paper from the ledger and handed it to Clay.

"He shook hands with the Grim Reaper. He's still weak as a mouse and it'll be a long time before he's able to return to work."

"What's the damage?" Clay asked as he looked at the slip of paper.

"Two bits. I'm surprised Mrs. Best is as healthy as she is. She's got the constitution of a horse."

"She's a surprising woman," Clay said as he dug the money from his pocket.

"*Gracias*," Teresa said with a giggle.

Clay took her by the arm and escorted her to the door, then paused to look back at Doctor Spencer.

"As far as Dave's concerned, maybe he shouldn't go back to being a lawman. Maybe he should let some younger pup take over."

"Maybe he should at that," Doctor Spencer said as Clay closed the door.

Chapter 21

"No, we didn't catch them, and it's my fault. I was the one who called off the chase."

Clay had been sitting on the porch in front of Dave King's house, relating to Dave and Roy what happened while they were chasing James Westfall and Curley. He stood as Maria and Teresa came from the house carrying mugs and a fresh pot of coffee.

"But didn't you and Julio have those children to take care of?" Maria asked, sitting the pot on a small wood table.

"Yeah, but that don't help much. We let 'em ride away pretty as you please."

"What kids?" Roy asked as Teresa handed him his coffee.

"My *marido muy fuerte* and Julio were close to catching them," Teresa said as she poured more coffee. "But *los bandidos* attacked a small *rancho*. They killed the children's mother and father, then wounded *Señor* Lincoln. They took their horses and rode away, while Clay and Julio looked after the children and bandaged *Señor* Lincoln."

"Who is *Señor* Lincoln." Dave's eyes darted between Clay and Teresa.

"He's the large black fellow drinking a beer out front of the saloon," Clay said. "He was sort of working for them folks Westfall killed. He says he came from the barn with a shotgun when they rode in, but one of them bored a hole in him, then killed the old man and woman."

Clay stepped down into the street and whistled loudly, before calling Joseph across the street.

"He's someone Roy needs to meet. He says he was a blacksmith before the war."

"Really? Why do I need to meet him?" Roy set his coffee mug down and stood as Joseph walked toward them.

"Well, you ain't fired the coals or fixed a thing since Dave got plugged. I'd kinda like my wagon wheel mended, and I'm sure Captain Ramos feels the same way."

"Joe," Clay said as Joseph stopped at the edge of the porch. "This is Sheriff Dave King."

"Sheriff," Joseph said with a nod.

"I'm sure he'd like to ask you a few questions about what took place."

"Ain't much to tell. Them men rode in and wanted the horses. Ol' man Diego took exception to it, because those horses belonged to the Mexican Federales."

"Federales? You didn't cross over into Mexico, did you?" Dave scrunched his brow.

"No, we were this side of the Rio," Clay said. "It wouldn't make any difference, would it?"

"I reckon not," Dave said with a snort. "They stole the horses. Then what?"

"Like I was saying, they weren't Diego's horses. The Federales were paying him stable fees for looking out for them. So, when he said no, they killed him and his wife, and shot me. Then, when I woke up, this fella and that Mexican pistolero were standing over me."

"And where were you all this time?" Dave asked Clay.

"Well, me and Julio were only minutes behind them. We heard the shots, but when we got there, the old man and woman were dead, and Westfall and his boys were gone. And, they had fresh horses."

"It ain't Mr. Best's fault none," Joe said. "Like he said, them men were on well fed, well rested military horses, while his horse was plum tuckered out. Besides, him and Julio had three children to look after. Ain't no way those two were gonna have a shoot-out when them children could get hurt."

"No, I suppose not. I would have done the same," Dave said and took a sip of coffee. "Maria? Would you please give Mr. Lincoln a cup?"

"*Si*, of course I will." She filled a mug, then offered Joe a seat.

"I hear you're handy with a forge and hammer," Roy said as Joe sat on the steps instead of the chair Maria had offered.

"A hammer and forge was all I knew before the war. I was fixin' to ask if I could fire up yours and fix Captain Ramos' wagon wheel that got busted in the Apache raid."

"Apache raid?" Dave and Roy asked in unison.

"What Apache raid?" Dave added.

"You'd have to ask Teresa 'bout that," Clay said. "It was all over and cleaned up by the time me and Julio rode in."

Clay quietly sipped his coffee as Teresa waved her arms and elaborated on the battle. He grinned, thinking this version was slightly larger and more exciting than the version he heard back in Cool Water. But, he reckoned, most battlefield tales grew in proportion of each telling. He was reminded near the end of the tale that Carol Jean had saved his daughter's life, and resolved to buy her a proper gift as soon as possible.

"And you're sure you want to live out there?" Dave asked as soon as Teresa finished her story.

"Ain't a whole lot more dangerous than living in town," Clay said with a snort. "You're the one sitting there covered with a blanket and hole in your back."

"I suppose, when you look at it that-a-way, you might be right." Dave grinned.

"As far as the forge and hammer," Roy said, to Joe, help yourself, but let me watch. If you're any good, I'd like to talk turkey with you. Maybe you can run the shop until Dave King is back on his feet."

"Not until he sees the doctor," Teresa said.

"I'm fine, Mrs. Best. See?" Joe moved his left arm in an arch.

"You are going to see Doctor Spencer, or I am going to get angry." Teresa glared at him.

"Better do what she says, Joe, or she's liable to get meaner than a hydrophobied skunk," Clay said with a chuckle.

"Yes, ma'am," Joe said with a nod. "I shore will go. Right after I finishes with my coffee."

Chapter 22

"It looks new," Jose Ramos said as he examined the repair on his wagon wheel. "What do I owe you?" He reached into his vest pocked to retrieve his wallet.

"You have to ask Mr. Johnson. I fixed it in his shop, and he offered me a job. So, I guess I work for him now," Joseph said.

"No charge," Roy said, with a shake of his head. "Teresa told us how you took charge during the Apache raid at Cool Water. So, this one's on the house."

Jose laughed. "Mrs. Best is too modest. I did rush to her house where the women and babies were, but Mrs. Best had already taken charge of defense. I fired my pistol like a good soldier, but she was the general. And it was Mrs. Mayfield who saved the babies when the warrior broke through the window."

"It doesn't matter who was the hero," Roy said. "What matters is that you and the other men and women were there to fight off the savages. The repair is still free."

******

Clay left the saloon carrying two mugs of cold beer and crossed the busy road toward the Sheriff's Office. He paused long enough to kick a wayward ball toward a gang of waiting children, then climb the steps to where Dave King was sitting on the porch that divided the residence from the office. He handed one mug to Dave and sat next to him, sipping his beer.

"Well, I filed a report saying I failed to catch Westfall and his gang."

"That's the rumor." Dave took a sip and wiped the foam from his moustache against his shirt sleeve. "Thanks for the beer."

"It's the least I could do, since those highbinders are runnin' loose."

"Oh, Christ have mercy," Dave said, crinkling his brow. "Don't tell me I've gotta listen to a bunch of nonsense from now on."

"It ain't no nonsense. I failed to drag them back here to hang. Least I coulda done was kill 'em."

"Well, it 'peers to me you had your hands full with those children and a wounded blacksmith. Wasn't much else you could do. Besides, you had Julio Garcia with you. I hear he didn't do much better."

"No, but it was my responsibility, and I failed."

"Oh, give it a rest. It's a wonder Teresa can stand being around you." Dave turned and yelled at the kitchen door. "Maria, could you come here a minute?"

She opened the door with flour up to her elbows.

"*Sí?*"

"Could you please fetch me my .45 so I can shoot this crybaby?"

"It ain't no laughing matter," Clay growled as Maria returned to the kitchen laughing. "James Westfall ain't done nothing but kill and hurt people since he's come back here, and someone's gotta stop him."

"And you think I don't know that? What happened to you out there? Did that big horse of yours kick you in the head?"

"No, but I had a bead on him with my Winchester and missed."

"Maybe." Dave took another sip. "But Teresa told Maria that you said that happened in the middle of that rain storm. She also said Westfall's horse stumbled the instant you pulled the trigger. Is that the way it happened?"

Clay didn't answer as he took a slow drink of the beer.

"It did come down that way, didn't it?"

"Well, yeah, pretty much."

"My hell, man!" Dave said with a laugh. "What'd you expect? You ain't God. You may think so, but you ain't."

"I'm not saying I'm God. All I'm saying is I failed. Plain and simple."

Clay raised his half-empty mug and spied a small group gathering at the base of the steps listening.

"What are y'all looking at? Git! All of you."

"No," Dave said. "I'm still sheriff here, and I say you all can stay. Stay and listen to Clay feel sorry for hisself."

"Not if they know what's good for them."

A couple of people cringed and slipped away, while the rest, including Roy Johnson, stayed.

"Dave's right, Clay," Roy said with a laugh. "No one's saying they could've done any better."

"Maybe so. But I ain't just anyone. Marshalling and upholding the law is all I've ever done. I should be better."

"Maria, where's that gun?" Dave yelled, and Roy laughed.

"You think it's funny?" Clay glared at Roy.

"No, Westfall and Curley ain't a laughing matter. But you're acting like an idgit."

"No one can catch every two-bit gunslinger and thief out there," Dave said. "I missed a few, and so have you. Even Wild Bill missed a couple of bad apples, and one of 'em bored a hole in the back of his head. So quit feeling sorry for yourself and get back out to your ranch. I hear it's quite a zoo now, and needs some tending."

Clay downed the last of his beer and snorted. "You don't know the half of it. It's full of Injuns and misfits. I kind of dread going back out there."

"A fellow that had been to California rode through last week," Roy said. "His horse had a loose shoe, so I hung up my gun long enough to help him out. He said there's a lot of good Indian *vaqueros* out there doing a fine job."

"Maybe, but those are different. Mine are Yaqui."

"They could be a handful, but that Federale said they got in there and fought the Apaches with everyone else. He said one of them died doing it."

"Yeah, a young boy trying to get to the stable. Teresa buried him next to Billy."

"Well, they might be useful."

"I ain't saying they can't be useful," Clay growled. "All I'm saying is, the place ain't turning out like I wanted. They've got houses and Indian huts scattered everywhere. They even built a dam across the creek, and now I've got a small lake just the other side of the stable."

"The way I see it, a lake might be a good thing during a drought, if it's got water in it." Dave chuckled.

"I ain't saying it's a bad thing. All I'm saying is, it ain't like I wanted. I would've put the dam farther down the creek, instead of so close."

"Yeah, and then you would've had to haul the water farther for the corral."

"You don't understand a thing I've said, do ya?"

"I understand you're upset because Teresa and the folks you left in charge actually took charge while you was gone, and got a few things done. Quit being an idgit, Clay. They coulda done nothing and left it all for you," Dave growled back.

"Look," he continued, "if you don't like the way things are going, tell 'em how you want it done. You ought to be thankful their still alive, instead of having their scalps hanging from some Apache's belt."

"I reckon you could be right, for once in your life," Clay said with a grin. "I reckon Teresa did hold things together while me and Julio were gone. And the dam was Theodore Russell's idea. Teresa's been trying hard to get them to stay, because they're farmers. She's got it in her head them staying and growing all kinds of things to eat."

"That's not a half-bad idea. Carrizo Springs could use some fresh vegetables, especially the way this drought's hanging on. Some of the stuff Maria brings home from the store looks like it belongs in a hog pen," Dave said. "I'd like to take a ride out there and see what's going on, as soon as the doc says it's okay."

"You're more'n welcome anytime. Bring Maria and the boys. I'll have one of them Yaquis butcher a calf and we'll roast it up. Now," Clay drained the last drop from his mug. "If you'll finish your beer, I'll take these mugs back to Charlie before he thinks we stole 'em."

Chapter 23

The sun had dipped low in the western sky, casting a red glow to a few scattered clouds. Gravel and sand crunched under the worn souls of James' boots as the three men limped toward the Rio Grande. Watching Clay Best ride away on his black horse and disappear behind a veil of rain had not set well with him. He ranted and called down curses on everyone and everything he could think of, especially the stolen horses that had spooked at the sound of thunder, taking everything, including the stolen money from Lehmann's Ranch. Now, his blistered feet inside the rain-soaked leather boots added to his misery.

"The peon's *casa* is this way," Carlos said as he pointed north.

"Yea, well there's no one there, 'cause we killed them," James growled.

"Maybe so, but it'll give us a place to spend the night," Curley said. "Might even find something to eat, if Clay didn't cart it off."

"Maybe." James limped over the small rise behind Carlos and stopped as the corral came into view. The horses they had been trying to find all day were inside the pen, still saddled. James seemed to explode and he charged the corral with gun drawn, calling the started animals every obscene name he could think of. It was Curley who caught him by the wrist and wrestled the weapon from his grasp.

"Hold on there, pard. If you shoot them horses, we'll be walking the rest of the way. I don't know about you, but I'm dog-tired of walking."

"Those sons-of-bitches deserve to die ... leaving us stranded all day."

"Well, let's get rested first. Then we'll ride somewhere there's better horses and you can shoot them if you want. But my feet's killing me," Curley said.

"Hey, *Jefe*," Carlos yelled from inside the corral. "The money is still here." He held up a fistful of Lehmann's money.

"Yea, that's where it's supposed to be," James growled.

"Yes it is, but you know how a horse can throw a pack when it's a runaway," Curley said, stuffing James gun back into its holster.

James nodded with a grunt as he entered the corral. He vaguely remembered Curley and Carlos discussing whether the horses might lose some of their packs, or if they'd ever find them. He uncorked his canteen and allowed some of the water to trickle down his parched throat before pouring a generous amount over his head.

"You know, *Jefe*," Carlos said after quenching his own thirst, "there is a small village across the Rio Grande, maybe four or five miles." He pointed north-west. "They have a small *cantina* with good food. I say we ride over there in the morning. Maybe take a bath, drink some *tequila* and *cerveza,* and get a good woman to keep us company. Eh, *Jefe*? Then, after we are rested, we'll go find this Clay Best and you can kill him. What do you say *Jefe*?"

"It isn't a bad idea," Curley said with a nod.

"You say they've got *cerveza* and women?" James asked.

"*Sí, Jefe*. The women there are ..." Carlos held his cupped hands as if he was fondling a woman's breast.

"Hell, these nags are rested enough. Let's go now," James said as he tightened the cinches on his saddle.

Chapter 24

Clay removed his hat and hung it on the rack as he entered the Cool Water Saloon. For some reason, while he was gone everyone had made the decision to eat their meals together as a group. Since the saloon was the only place large enough to accommodate that many people at one time, the Cool Water Saloon had become a cafe. He sat next to Teresa as Rob made the rounds served heaping spoonfuls of rice and beans on each plate. One of the Yaqui girls followed a few steps behind with slices of roasted elk, while an even younger girl followed with a platter of hot tortillas. He understood, from Teresa, that the girls were sisters, and it was their father who had killed the animal that very morning. The elk had spent most of the day on a spit over a smoldering mesquite fire.

"Well, that critter isn't going to last long amongst this crowd," Clay said with a chuckle.

"I don't think it was meant to," Teresa said. "It is their way of saying welcome home. They are happy we returned safely."

"Well, tell him he's welcome."

Clay took a forkful of rice and beans as Teresa approached a stern-looking middle-aged Yaqui sitting at the next table. The man's eyes locked on Clay as she gave him the message. The Yaqui gave Clay a nod of recognition, which he returned. He took a bite of elk as Teresa returned to her seat.

"This is pretty good," he mumbled while chewing.

"*Sí*, Rob checked on the elk throughout the day, adding some of the spices I told him about.

"It's all good. The rice and beans, everything. You taught him well."

"*Gracias*." Teresa smiled and shifted in her chair to study him. "That was very nice."

"I meant it. The boy may be a farmer, but he'd make a hell of a cook in a restaurant somewhere."

The girl with the tortillas stopped by his chair and Clay took two before patting her on the head. "Thank you, darlin'."

The girl was missing her front teeth and gave him a toothless smile.

"I think my husband is getting to like these Indians, isn't he?"

"I reckon they're just folks like the rest of us." He reached for the bottle of wine and filled both their cups. "There's probably good and bad Yaqui the same as there's good and bad white folks. So far, I'd say we got some good ones. Are they gonna stick around and do some farming?"

"Estrella's uncle said that would depend on how often the Apache attack. If they come again, they will find a safer place to live."

"I can understand that, but I'd think they're safer here, with us having guns to fight back," Clay said. "Especially if Theodore decides to stay. I think the Apaches might be a little shy about that buffalo gun he's got."

He took another bite of rice and beans, then washed it down with a sip of wine.

"Have they decided anything yet?"

Teresa twirled her cup of wine and heaved a sigh. "I don't think they will stay. Rob's wife doesn't like it here."

Clay glanced toward Clara seated at a neighboring table next to her mother. She was trying to rock her baby and eat at the same time.

"Huh, I don't think I've said two words to her after saying thanks for saving Yolanda's life. I gave her a little hug, but that's about it."

"Maybe you should tell her how you really feel, whether she stays or goes."

"Excuse me," Clay said in a booming voice as he stood. The room grew quiet and he cleared his voice.

"It 'peers to me I've failed to thank some folks. First of all, I need to thank Clara Jean for saving Yolanda when the Apache's attacked. I wasn't around to look after her, and I don't know what we'd do if we had lost her."

"You don't need to thank me, Mr. Best," Clara said quietly.

"I reckon I do. And I need to thank a whole lot of folks. Y'all pitched in and took charge when the chips were down. All of you fought off the Apaches. And I come back and see houses all over the place. I even have a lake that I didn't have when I left, thanks to Theodore. Most of all, I've never thanked my wife, Teresa, and told her how much I appreciate her taking over a big job of running this ranch while I was gone. She did it without complaining, and did a better job that I did while I was here."

He paused and took a sip of wine as Theodore and Hildegarde led the room in applause.

"That's all I wanted to say. Y'all can eat."

He sat down and Teresa leaned forward to kiss him. "Thank you my *marido muy fuerte*. I am the lucky one to have you."

"I reckon I'm the lucky one. I still don't understand why you'd want to marry an old crusty coot like me. All I know is chasing crooks and killers. I still don't know if I'll make a good rancher or not. You might have to tell me what to do."

Teresa laughed and kissed him again.

"I don't think I'll have any trouble doing that, my love. I do that anyway."

They turned in their chairs as Clara pulled a chair to their table and sat down. She took a deep breath and exhaled.

"Thank you for the things you said. But please don't make me into some hero, 'cause I ain't." She shook her head slowly. "I've already told folks here that I was scared to death when those savages attacked. I still am. It was Mrs. Best and Captain Ramos that kept things together."

"Well, from what I hear, everyone did their part, including you," Clay said, squeezing her arm. "And it ain't a crime to be scared. I'm sure everyone was."

"That's what Captain Ramos keeps saying, but if Mrs. Best was scared, it sure didn't show. My hands were shaking so hard, I had trouble loading the gun. And I still don't know how I managed to shoot that man. It just happened."

"It's that way with everyone," Clay said with a chuckle.

"Even you?"

"Oh, hell yeah. Pardon my language, but I'm always afraid when it comes to gunplay. There's always the chance of getting shot. You'd be a fool not to be afraid of an Apache warrior. The key is to keep your wits about you."

"How do you do that?" Clara wiped the corner of her eye with her knuckles.

"It just happens. Experience, mainly," Clay said and took a sip of wine. "And it doesn't hurt to say a quick prayer."

"Do you pray?"

"Never know when you're gonna meet your maker, and it doesn't hurt to be on speaking terms with him."

"I'm still scared out of my wits, thinking I'll wake up in the morning staring into the face of an Apache who's got my baby."

"That's understandable, *chica*." Teresa hugged her.

"How do you do it? How can you live way out here, miles from anyone? I'd go crazy with fear."

"You lived on a farm, didn't you?" Clay asked.

"Yes, but that was different. We had neighbors all around us. There's nothing out here, except cattle and sage brush."

"I reckon ranch life ain't for everyone. Maybe you should tell your husband that."

"I did, and he just shrugs and says you folks need him. He likes fixing big meals to feed everyone. I think it makes him feel important."

Teresa and Clay looked at each other quietly for a few seconds before Teresa grinned and said, "Can you talk to Rob for me?"

"Consider it done. And, as for you, young lady," Clay laid a hand on Clara's shoulder, "I'd quit thinking of myself as a coward and learn how to defend yourself and that baby, no matter where you put down roots. I hear some folks are shooting and killing each other in California as well as anywhere else. Maybe you'd feel safer in town where there's lots of folks around."

"Mrs. Best says you taught her how to shoot. Can you teach me?"

"I suppose so. First thing is to get you the right gun. I promised Captain Ramos I'd see if there's any property for sale hereabouts, but Henry Jenkins, the fellow who runs the bank, was in San Antonio on business. So, I need to run back to Carrizo Springs in a few days and see what's for sale. Why don't you and Rob come along and we'll see if Hans has anything that fits your fancy."

"He's the man who owns the gun store," Teresa explained.

"Oh, okay," Clara said with a nod.

******

The supper inside the saloon evolved into a small *fiesta* outdoors, with singing and dancing around a bonfire. Theodore produced a fiddle from the back of their wagon and Teresa joined Juanita Ramos, Rebecca Santiago and Estrella in a traditional Mexican folk dance. It didn't take long before Captain Ramos and Leo joined them. Clay disappeared inside the saloon and returned with a bottle of wine and a bottle of brandy. He gave the Indians each a small cup of wine, then raised his eyebrows when one of them produced a jug of mescal and began passing it around. He braced himself for trouble, but it turned out that the Yaqui showed great restraint in their drinking.

"My uncle and grandmother will not tolerate drunkenness among their family," Estrella said. "Anyone who gets intoxicated is punished severely."

Clay nodded his approval, knowing there had been a few times he would have failed that standard miserably.

It was approaching midnight when he crept inside the house. It took several seconds before his eyes became accustomed to the darkness. The children were sleeping soundly, with Yolanda cuddled next to Isabel. Clara's visit to their table had somehow given permission to nearly everyone one inside the saloon to do the same. By the time he had finished his meal, it had turned to cold elk with cold rice and beans. Teresa appeared to be asleep, so he removed his boots and stripped down to his long johns before slipping into bed next to her. She immediately pulled him close and placed her warm lips against his ear.

"Thank you so much for being patient with her."

"Who?" he asked in a hoarse whisper. "Clara Jean?"

"*Sí*, she needs your help."

"What she needs is a swift kick in the bloomers."

"I think the same sometimes. But she is frightened and needs to learn to be strong. Be kind with her."

The feel of her warm breath and lips caused his body to react in a familiar way. He tried moving to a different position, but she wrapped an arm around him pulling him even closer.

"Okay, but you'd best let go of me."

"Why? Is my husband feeling warm inside?"

"Your husband is feeling a might more than warm."

"Good." She ran the tip of her tongue across his ear.

"Lord have mercy, woman." He breathed heavily. "You know what the doc said."

"Yes, and I also know my own body." She explored his body with her hands as she rolled him to his back.

Clay started to push her away when she slid her tongue inside his mouth. That's when he quit fighting and allowed her to have her way. He lay exhausted and sweaty by the time they finished. He rolled to look at the children and was amazed that they had stayed asleep. If being nice to Clara Jean Mayfield was all it took, he vowed to become the nicest man in in the state of Texas.

Chapter 25

It was dark when Westfall and his companions road their tired horses down the one and only street in Agua Mala. It wasn't really a street by any stretch of the imagination in James' mind. Just a dirt road, cluttered with horse droppings, that divided the few buildings that made up the town. There was a small corral and stable, a store, several *jacales* and a *cantina*, the *cantina* being the largest of the buildings.

Dismounting at the stable, James took a sip of water from the bucket fastened to a rope at the well and discovered how the village earned the name "Bad Water." The water was thick with alkali.

"Gawd," he spit and wiped his mouth against his sleeve. "How do the horses stand to drink that stuff?"

"Think I'll wait and have a beer," Curley said with a laugh.

James gave the old *peon* a gold coin, then warned him to take care of the animals and their tack, or he'd pay with his life. He then divided the money they had taken from Lehmann's Ranch. He cursed loudly when the final tally was taken. They had been shot at and chased across the border into Mexico for less than six-hundred dollars. He screamed his curses toward the sky, wishing he'd killed every dog on that ranch. He figured if they hadn't started barking, he would have found where Lehmann kept his real money.

"Hey, *Jefe*," Carlos said. "Let's go drink some *tequila* and find a woman."

James growled as he followed Carlos and Curley into the *cantina*. His mood improved when he found the *cerveza* and *tequila* quite tasty.

The building was filled with dusty vaqueros and whores. An old man sat on a wicker chair against the back wall playing guitar. James was almost positive the whores occupied the *jacales*, but the vaqueros must have come from local farms, or perhaps they were on the run like he was, and using Agua Mala as a stop-over.

Carlos leaned across the bar and said something to the bartender, who nodded and disappeared into the back room, then returned moments later with a plate piled high with beans and cheese rolled tightly inside hot flour tortillas. James' stomach growled instantly as he reached for one of the tortillas. The hot beans and cheese burnt his mouth, but the flavor was even better than the beer he washed it down with. Several more tortillas and beers and Clay Best had become a faint memory stuck somewhere in the back of his mind. A chunky whore brushed her breasts against him as she leaned toward the bar to retrieve a shot of *tequila*. On a whim, he grabbed and kissed her.

"*Hola*," she said with a smile. "Are you lonely, big man?"

"I'll say. I ain't been with a woman in so long, my horse is startin' to look interesting."

James half expected her to start purring as she rubbed her body against his.

"Then maybe we should do something about that. Do you want me, *hombre* ?"

"Yeah, you'll do just fine. How much?"

" *Cinco pesos*, or *quince pesos por* all night.

"Would this do?" James handed her a gold coin.

"*Señor*, I take special care of you."

She took hold of his hand and led him through the door and toward the nearest *jacale*."

******

True to her word, Edita, if that was her real name, proved to be more than adequate as a lover, and had hardly left his side the entire week. She kept a fresh drink on the table while he played poker and made sure he had a hot meal when his stomach growled. It didn't matter, mid-afternoon of middle of the night, she climbed into his bed and left him sweat-soaked and weak as a kitten.

They had been in Agua Mala a little over a week when James looked inside his billfold to discover his share of the money was almost gone. He had kept track of the billfold, and was certain it wasn't due to theft. He was also sure Edita had not taken any. The fact was, she had flown into a rage only yesterday when the owner of the store tried to over-charge him on a new shirt. But buying three meals a day for Edita and himself, as well as drinks at the *cantina* and poker stakes, had taken its toll.

"How much you got left?" he asked as Curley paid for a couple of drinks.

"Mostly gone. How about you?"

"The same." James took a swallow of beer and burped. "You seen Carlos anywhere?"

"Not since yesterday. Why?"

"The thing is, we still owe that peon at the stable a week's boarding for the horses, and we gotta eat. So, unless Carlos is well fixed, we're gonna have to go back to work."

"Well, he's been hanging out with that young whore he latched onto first night here. I think he's been living with her. I understand her folks have a small farm outside of town."

James laughed. "Hell, as small as this place is, that might be ten feet away."

"I'll ask Rose where they've been staying."

Curley took one the drinks to a heavily painted prostitute and kissed her on the cheek. After talking to her for a minute, he returned with a grin.

"She says they are still together, and she'll take us to their place in a few minutes."

******

A scantily-clad young girl, who James guessed might be about twelve, answered when he knocked on the door.

"You understand English?" he asked.

"*Sí*," she said with a nod.

"Is a *vaquero* named Carlos been staying here?"

"*Sí*." She turned to yell, "Carlos, these men want to see you."

Carlos came to the door barefoot and bare-chested, holding his gun.

"*Jefe*! Curley!" Carlos visibly relaxed. "*¿Qué es, Jefe*? You having a good time?"

He opened the door wide and allowed them to step inside the small, one-room house. An old grey-headed woman was busy peeling potatoes with a short-bladed knife at the table. She locked eyes with James and never took them off, watching his every move. Two small children were playing with toy animals made from dried corncobs underneath the table. The young prostitute sat in the only chair and hiked her dress, displaying her wares.

"Yeah, I've been actually having a great time."

"*Bueno*," Carlos said with a laugh. "Chica has been showing me a great time also."

The girl cocked her head to one side and smiled as she hiked her dress even higher. She wasn't wearing anything underneath the thin dress.

"What me and Curley came for was to see how you're fixed. We're running kind of low on money."

"Oh, *Jefe*, the money, it is gone. I only have a few pesos. Chica's mother is sick and they needed the money more than those in the *cantina*. That's why I've been staying here."

"Yeah, you don't need to tell me. That's what I expected," James said with a laugh. "It's time to go back to work. Me and Curley will wait outside while you say your goodbyes."

Carlos was pulling on his boots when James stepped outside and closed the door.

"Hell, if he gave that old woman two-hundred American dollars, I'll bet she made that girl show him a great time," Curley said.

"Yeah, but I don't think I could do anything with that old gal and them young-uns watching.

******

It was approximately twelve o'clock noon when they rode out of Agua Mala and headed toward the border. The old peon had taken care to make sure their horses were well-fed and rested. After spending a week with Edita, James felt he was ready for anything, including settling the score with Clay Best.

Chapter 26

"Please have a seat, gentlemen, both of you." Henry Jenkins opened his office door to yell at his teller as Clay and Jose sat in two over-stuffed chairs.

"James, please bring Captain Ramos and Mr. Best cups of coffee!"

"Yes sir, Mr. Jenkins, right away."

"Well now, what can I do for you gentlemen? Henry Jenkins said as he seated himself behind the oak desk and shuffled some paper to make a clean spot. Clay always considered the large desk rather pretentious, and the size only gave Henry more space to spread his clutter.

"We was wanting to see if there's any land for sale hereabouts," Clay said.

"Oh, yes, I remember Captain Ramos saying he is looking to purchase some land," Henry said.

They paused as James delivered two steaming cups of coffee.

"I know Mr. Best likes his coffee black, but I forgot to ask, Captain Ramos, if you'd like anything in your coffee. Sugar or cream?"

"Oh no," Jose said with a chuckle. "We never had such luxuries in the army. Black is fine. *Gracias.*"

James smiled with a nod and stepped out of the office, closing the door.

"Well, with the drought we've been having, you can almost have your pick of land," Henry said as he pulled a folder from a file cabinet. He laid the file on the desk and smiled.

"Boy, wasn't that storm we had last week a welcome sight?"

"You didn't get caught out in it," Clay said with a chuckle.

"No, but I don't think I would have minded. In fact, I did stand out in the street a few minutes just to say 'thank you Lord.' We need quite a bit more."

He ran his finger down the page and paused with a grin.

"The old Hillmire spread, just west of your place, Mr. Best, is going up for auction in two weeks. It's quite a bit smaller than the Cool Water Ranch, but it's got a year-around spring, house, barn and fencing."

"Yeah, I've seen it. It's nice enough. How many acres goes with it?" Clay asked.

"According to the survey, it's right at three-hundred acres, touching your Cool Water ranch."

"Three hundred acres is more than I can take care of by myself," Jose said with a chuckle. "I'm looking for something a little smaller."

"Don't turn it down so quick," Clay said. "I've seen it, and it's a real nice spread."

"And what would I do with that much land?"

"I'll rent what you don't use. You could also buy a few head and let 'em range on Cool Water property, if you want."

"Well, it looks like Clay's already been thinking this through," Henry said with a chuckle.

"No, it just makes sense," Clay said. "Captain Ramos and his wife need a place of their own, and you'd be hard pressed to find a nicer place in these parts. I was thinking about it for me and Teresa, but I kinda owe Jose a lot. So, I figure it's payback time."

"Thank you, but I don't have a lot of money. It will depend on what Mr. Jenkins thinks the rancho will sell for at the closing bid," Jose said.

"Well now, that's anyone's guess," Henry arched his eyebrows and cocked his head. "The bank in Austin tried auctioning off a fairly nice farm last week, and absolutely no one placed bid on the property."

"No one?" Clay said.

"No one," Henry repeated. "I guess folks are gun-shy due to the drought. I'd like to give you an educated guess, but I'm afraid that's not possible. I'd just show up and stay in the bidding as long as you're able. The only stickler is, it's an all-cash sale. The creditor will not issue credit."

"What if a fella got a loan from your bank prior to the sale? Would that work?" Clay said.

"If you're asking if Captain Ramos presents a bank-guaranteed loan to cover the sales price of the land ... yes, I believe that would work," Henry said with a nod of his balding head.

"That brings me to another question," Clay said. "What if he comes up a little shy for the down payment on the loan? Is my credit strong enough to back a loan on the place?"

"No, I couldn't let you do that," Jose said, shaking his head.

"Why not? I ain't planning on giving it to you. Besides, I'd rather have you there than some highbinder complaining 'bout my cows on his property, or maybe stealing them." Clay crossed his arms and frowned.

"I'm afraid you'll have to work that out between yourselves before the auction. In the meantime ..." Henry closed the folder and shoved it back in the file. "To answer your question, yes. Your credit is good with me, although you've been spending a lot of money this past year. I'm not complaining, mind you. All I'm saying is, your bank account isn't what it used to be."

"Am I broke?"

"No, far from it."

"Then I could back his loan, if I wanted to."

"Yes, Mr. Best, you certainly could."

"Much obliged." Clay shook Henry's hand and ushered Jose out of the bank and toward the saloon.

"I will not allow you to do such a thing," Jose said as they reached the bat wing doors.

"What?" Clay stopped with one hand on the swinging door. "Buy you a drink?"

"No, sign for my loan."

"We can discuss that over a drink." Clay pushed the door, but Jose pulled it back.

"We will not discuss it at all."

"Okay, you buy the first drink."

Clay pushed the door wide and entered the saloon. The place was almost empty, with only four men playing cards at a table against the opposite wall. Clay reached the bar and looked around.

"Where's Charlie?"

"He's out back trying his hand at cooking," one of the men at the table said. "Ol' Frank here made the mistake of saying he was hungry. Now, he's gonna pay the price."

"What happened to Juan?" Clay asked.

"He quit," Frank said. "He got offered a job by some fancy restaurant in San Antone, and Charlie wouldn't give him a raise, so he quit."

"Can't blame him none. He had a wife and four young-uns to feed," one of the other men said."

"Well, I don't reckon he'll mind if we help ourselves," Clay said, rounding the bar. "Anyone care for a refill?"

"Sure, we can stand one. Frank's stack of chips is smaller than the rest, so he can get the drinks," George said.

"Don't you worry 'bout my chips," Frank said as he turned his cards face down and piled some chips on top. "I've got a real good hand going."

"Shore you do," George said.

"That's what you said last hand," said a man Clay knew as Montana.

Frank carried their empty mugs to the bar and Clay filled them with beer. He then filled two shot glasses with *tequila*, and two more mugs with beer.

"How about that table over yonder?" Clay nodded his head toward the far corner table.

"You may take your pick of tables," Jose said with a chuckle.

"Well, here's mud in your eye," Clay said, and toasted Jose with the *tequila*.

"Ha!" Frank yelled as he spread his cards. "I told you I had a good hand." He raked the pile of chips toward himself and began counting.

"Well, we had to let you win at least one hand, or you'd quit playing," George said.

A loud bang came from the kitchen followed by a string of curses.

"Hell, it's good we let him win," Montana said. "From the sound of it, he shore ain't gonna eat nothing."

Charlie Roberts came from the kitchen with his right hand wrapped in a wet towel. His white apron was splattered with red sauce.

"What happened?" Clay asked over the mug of beer.

"Burnt my hand on that damned frying pan."

"*Sí*, they do get hot," Jose said with a chuckle.

Sorry you hurt yourself," George said. Clay caught sight of a crooked grin in the corner of George's mouth as he dealt another hand.

"You're gonna have to hire another cook like Juan, if you plan on serving food," Montana said with a snort. "Clay had to fetch us beers while you were back there in the kitchen gettin' burnt up."

"Money's on the bar," Clay said, and took a sip.

"Much obliged, Clay," Charlie said, then turned to stare at him from across the bar.

"Wasn't Teresa wanting to run the kitchen here once upon a time?"

"Yeah, way back before we got married. But we've got a baby now, and live at Cool Water. So, if you're thinking of asking her to come work here, you've got another think coming. The answer's no."

"Can she cook?" George asked.

"Shore, she can cook," Charlie said. "Would I be asking if she didn't?"

"Maybe. You refused to pay Juan enough to keep him."

"That's 'cause egg-heads like you said you wouldn't pay more for good food." Charlie threw a wadded-up bar towel at him that fell several feet short.

"We never said that a'tall," Frank said.

"All we said was, the food was gonna have to be good, if you was gonna start charging more," George said.

"Well, why didn't you say so, before Juan quit?"

"How in the hell was we supposed to know Juan was gonna quit?" Montana said.

"You was his boss. You shoulda knowed better," Frank growled.

"Well, I didn't," Charlie snapped.

"Better start looking, then," Montana said with a snicker.

Charlie turned back toward Clay and stopped as Clay toasted him with the beer mug.

"You heard the man, Charlie. Better start looking."

Clay laughed and turned toward Jose.

"Whadda ya think, captain? How about us packing our wives into a buggy with a picnic lunch, and going to see the place before making any decisions?"

"*Sí*," Jose said with a nod. "Either way, it won't be half as much fun as watching your friend Charlie."

Jose toasted Clay with his mug and laughed.

Chapter 27

"It is very pretty," Juanita Ramos said as she viewed the rambling ranch home from the buggy. The main quarters of the stone and mortar structure was in the form of an L, with a smaller section of guest quarters added later, making a lopsided U.

Jose helped Juanita and Teresa from the buggy as Clay searched for the key ring Henry had loaned them and unlocked the front door. The house was dark and smelled of dust.

"How long has it been vacant?" Teresa asked as she pulled back the shutters and opened a window.

"Henry said most of a month," Clay said. "The bank took it over a couple of weeks ago."

"It certainly is big enough," Juanita said. Her high-top laced shoes clicked against the stone floor as she opened another window.

"Oh, my!" Teresa said as she entered the kitchen.

"What is it?" Juanita asked.

"Look," Teresa said, running her fingers across the large wood-burning stove.

"Huh," Clay said. "Guess the Hillmires figured that thing was too big and heavy to move."

"I don't blame them," Jose said with a chuckle.

"I've never had a kitchen this size," Juanita said, trailing her fingers across the cast iron sink. She stopped to stare at the small pump. "Does that work?" she asked, staring at Jose.

"According to Henry, I reckon it does," Clay said. He grabbed the handle and gave several pumps before a gush of water spilled into the sink, causing the ladies to squeal.

Both women disappeared quickly down the hall, examining each room as they went.

"Well, I reckon it doesn't take much to make a woman happy," Clay said with a chuckle. "I wouldn't have given that pump a second thought."

"That's because we weren't the ones hauling water to cook and wash dishes," Jose said. He pulled two cigars from his vest pocket and handed one to Clay.

"I reckon not. Although," Clay said as he lit the cigar, "I did my share the last month Teresa was pregnant. Then, I did 'em a while longer after little Yolanda was born, until she was back on her feet."

"I was luckier," Jose said with a grin. "I was able to get Juanita a young servant girl to do those things.

"Wouldn't that be sweet?" Clay said with a nod. "Don't know if that'd be possible for me. Teresa's pretty set in her ways, and she'd probably run the girl off if she didn't do things a certain way."

They followed the women as they bounced from room to room, finally ending outdoors in the small court yard.

"You could put a small table and chairs over here and watch the sunset as you drink your evening coffee," Teresa said.

"I would probably eat breakfast here too, on warm mornings," Juanita said.

The baby woke from her nap and began wailing.

"Yes, I know," Teresa said with a coo. "You need to be changed and you're hungry."

Juanita followed Teresa toward the buggy, chattering about the house.

"Well, I reckon we got a few minutes to kill. Let's take a look at the spring," Clay said.

They found the small spring at the back of the house tucked in the middle of a grove of mesquite and wild flowers. The water gurgled from a rocky shelf, forming a small pond. A creek of amber water trailed merrily from the pond southward toward the Rio Grande, leaving a trail of green grass, lined with mesquite and brush.

Clay knelt by the rock shelf, cupping his hand to take a sip from the spring. He gave Jose a nod and smiled.

"Good water. Not a taste of alkali."

Jose followed suit and nodded his agreement.

"It is good. I wonder why they would leave a place like this."

"My guess is, while this spring is a good one, it isn't enough to support three-hundred acres." Clay walked away from the house and surveyed the land.

"See, everything's burnt up, except for right here, near the spring. It's too dry to farm or support cattle, until it starts raining again."

He turned back to Jose.

"On the other hand, there's plenty of water to have a nice sized garden and raise a few head. And like I said, you could range a few head on my place, if you wanted."

"It is possible," Jose said thoughtfully. There might be a way to grow a few acres of corn, tomatoes and chilis. It is a large house. Might be too large for Juanita to take care of."

"Don't sell that woman short, Captain," Clay said with a laugh. "I think she's a might tougher than you think. Besides," he removed his hat and wiped the band. "You said your son and his family were about to starve to death on the family spread. You can send for them and they can give you a hand, until the drought lifts."

Jose laughed and shook his head.

"You should go into politics. I think you could easily be elected governor ... maybe even president. I'll discuss it with Juanita and let you know."

Chapter 28

The mule-drawn stage rumbled over the trail toward Uvalde, leaving a cloud of dust in its wake. They were approaching an outcropping of rock where the road turned as it crested a small hill, forcing the stage to slow. The perfect spot for a holdup, and several would-be bandits had made a try in years past. One such thief had severely wounded an armed guard, almost killing him.

"Better keep an eye out," Miles Sorenson said as he pulled back on the reins and pressed on the brake lever with his right foot. Miles was a five year veteran driver for Wells Fargo, and had been an experienced teamster before hiring on.

"I'm watching," Gopher Tucker said as he adjusted his grip on the carriage gun. Gopher had gotten his nickname from his large buck-teeth. He was also a seasoned veteran of the stage line and was considered one of the best armed guards Wells Fargo had.

The mules slowed their gait and easily crested the hill. The stage made the turn and Miles released his breath as the mules regained their stride and the stage picked up speed. Gopher also relaxed some, as the worst was past. They were passing the last of the rocks when a man appeared to Gopher's right and fired a Winchester. The .45 slug slammed into Gopher's temple, showering Miles in blood. An instant later, a second man appeared to Miles' left, also with a

Winchester. The bullet hit Miles' chest with a thud. The last thing Miles remembered was feeling like he's been hit by a boulder as he catapulted from the stage to the ground, then … nothing.

Carlos galloped onto the road, grabbing the lead mule's reins and slowing the stage. Curley leaped from the rocks and trotted toward the stage. He dove for cover once again as someone inside the stage opened fire, almost hitting him. He returned fire and James Westfall joined in on the opposite side, quitting only when the Winchesters were empty.

Both men approached the stage with caution. Carlos joined them, with his pistol drawn. Curley opened one of the doors to reveal two dead men, three dead women, and one small girl, holding a blood-soaked doll. Carlos holstered his gun with a curse, then began saying a Rosary over the dead child.

"Hell, I keep forgetting Carlos wasn't in the war," James said with a laugh.

"I see things," Carlos snapped. "She's so young."

"Yeah, but one of the men in our outfit got his guts blown out by a ten-year-old boy. When it comes to guns and shooting, they're all the same in my book," Curley said.

"This is what Captain Quantrill used to call *collateral* damage," James said with a snicker. "We used to see dead young'uns all the time. Sometimes it was the Yankees that killed 'em … sometimes one of us. It didn't matter who fired the shot. If they got in the way of a bullet, they died."

James rolled a smoke. "If you don't like seeing the girl, jump up there and toss the strongbox down. Curley and me will see what these folks got on 'em."

The passengers combined were carrying seventy-five dollars in bills and change, as well as a couple of wedding rings and a gold locket and chain. Curley shot the lock off the strongbox and they pulled another eight-hundred dollars in cash and coin.

"Well, it ain't as much as I was hoping, but it still ain't bad for a day's work," James said. He motioned toward Carlos as he stuffed his share into his saddlebags.

"Climb up on them rocks and take a look-see if anyone's coming."

Carlos made short work of climbing the rocks and turned in a slow circle.

"No, *Jefe*, I see nobody."

"Good. Let's get packed and ride outta here."

James grinned and crushed his smoke under the toe of his boot.

"Anyone got any preferences where we go?"

Carlos shrugged. " Agua Mala was nice."

"Yeah, I thought you'd say that," James said with a snicker. "That young whore wouldn't have anything to do with it, would she?"

"Maybe," Carlos admitted.

"I didn't have such luck," Curley said, "but I did have myself a good time. Doesn't make any never-mind to me."

James stared thoughtfully toward the horizon, wondering if it might be possible to hook up with Edita once more. He turned toward Carlos and laughed.

"Okay, let's head toward Agua Mala."

Chapter 29

"I'm not set on staying, but I still don't understand what you've got against it." Rob crinkled his brow and glared at Clara as he pulled off his boots. "I thought you were over being jealous about my relationship with Mrs. Best."

"It ain't that," Clara snapped. "I am over that … mostly. We're friends now, and she's been teaching me some things."

"What is it, then?" Rob stood and removed his suspenders, then began unbuttoning his pants.

Clara sat on the edge of the bed and hiked her skirt to remove her stockings. William had been fed and was sleeping soundly in his cradle in the corner of the tiny room.

"It's just that … just that it's so desolate. We ain't got a neighbor within miles."

"Clara Jean," Rob said gently. "We were living on a cotton farm back in Pittsburg, and we didn't have any real close neighbors."

"We had two neighbors, Effie Jones and Harold Baker. they lived close enough to walk to, if you wanted," Clara said. She stuffed the stockings inside her lace-up shoes and turned her back toward him as she unbuttoned her blouse.

Rob hung his pants and shirt on the wooden chair before slipping his arms around her.

"Here, let me do that," he said softly in her ear.

Clara tilted her head to see him.

"I can unbutton my blouse."

"I know you can, but I want to do it tonight.

"Be quiet. William ..."

"I'll be quiet."

She leaned against him as his fingers undid the buttons, then slowly peeled the blouse open. She took in a shaky breath as Rob's fingers trailed across her chemise, lingering slightly longer at each breast.

"If you don't really want to stay here, we can make other plans, regardless of what your parents decide."

"Really?"

"Yes, really."

He finished pulling off her blouse and tossed it on top of his clothes. Then he unbuttoned her skirt and let it fall. "It's just that the Indians… What if there had been more?"

"Shhhh," he whispered in her ear. "There's no Indians here now, only me. And we'll sit down tomorrow and figure what we're going to do, together."

Clara tilted her head to see his face as her chemise top fell. "Real....?"

The question fell short as Rob pressed his lips against hers. He gently eased her to the bed and removed the bloomers, tossing them toward the chair.

"My nightgown … "

"You won't need it tonight."

Rob removed his long johns and climbed in beside her, pulling her body next to his.

"Tonight, it's just you and me, getting to know each other better."

Clara caught her breath as he explored her ear with his tongue. Thoughts of Apache warriors and the isolation of the Cool Water ranch vanished as Rob's hands explored her body. Tomorrow and all its problems were another day.

Chapter 30

Ray King buckled the gun belt around his hips and adjusted it before tying the leather thong around his right leg. The weight of the Colt felt familiar, like an old friend. He checked the loads in the revolver before dropping it back into its holster.

"You didn't listen to a word I said last night, did you?"

Ray glanced up as Maria folded her arms across her chest and glared from the kitchen.

"Yes, I did," he said with a nod. "But, as far as I know, I'm still sheriff, and I have a job to do. Election is next month and the town can elect someone different, if they want to."

"Are you going to run? They'll elect you, if you do. You know that, don't you?"

"Yeah, I suppose so."

Ray crossed the room and placed his hands on her shoulders. He pulled her against his chest as a tear trickled from the corner of her right eye.

"Maria, I don't know how to do anything else. I was a deputy in Piedras Negras by the time I was fifteen. I came here as sheriff when Kirby Johnson got killed during the war. This is all I've ever done."

"Clay and Teresa are doing something different. We could too."

"Clay and Teresa had the money to do what they're doing. We don't."

"Teresa said they would help us." Maria stared up into his face and more tears spilled over.

"I'm not going to become a charity case, Maria, and I'm too proud to beg."

He gave her a quick kiss and turned toward the door.

"I'll be careful. I promise." She was crying openly when he pulled the door closed.

Ray consoled the pain inside his chest with the knowledge that she would get used to his being sheriff once again as time went by. Besides, he reasoned, he'd known plenty of ranchers who had been killed or crippled by being thrown from a horse, or gored by a bull, or even scalped by an Indian. And those that did live to a ripe old age were mostly crippled and not able to enjoy their twilight years No, he thought, he'd rather go in a blaze of gunfire when his time was up.

He crossed the street at an angle, waving to Joseph Lincoln and Roy Johnson at the blacksmith shop. He stopped at Carson's General Store and gave his hat a tip as Gertie Blankenship exited, carrying a baby in one arm and a basket of dry goods in the other.

"Ma'am. How's little Crawford this morning?"

"He didn't sleep too well last night, Sheriff. Teething, you know. I see you're back on the job. Are you feeling strong enough?"

"Yes ma'am, I am. Thank you for asking."

He held the door open and waited until she had gone a ways down the wooden walkway before entering the store. He'd make his usual rounds, talking to people and letting them know he was back on the job. Whether it was a buried fear or pure caution, he didn't know, but he found himself constantly glancing over his shoulder and making sure his back was not toward a doorway or window. He swore to himself he'd never make that mistake again, *so help me God.*

Chapter 31

The auction of the Hillmire ranch went quickly, with only four others bidding. It didn't seem to Clay as if the other bidders were even interested in buying the ranch, since two each placed only one bid. Another dropped out on the third bid. According to Henry Jenkins, the remaining buyer was a banker from San Antonio who wanted to buy the property on speculation. He believed it could sell for a substantial profit once the drought ended. Captain Ramos stayed in the bidding at Clay's urging, forcing the banker to quit on the sixth bid.

"Well, it looks as though you bought yourself three hundred acres of prime Texas land," Henry said, shaking Captain Ramos' hand. "I'll see you two and your wives in town this afternoon to sign the legal papers."

"Is it really true?" Juanita said, slipping her arm around Jose's left arm. "Do we own this rancho?"

"Yes, we will once we sign the papers. We also owe *Señor* Clay and his wife a sizeable amount of money. I have no idea how we are going to pay them back."

"Don't worry about that," Teresa said. "We can discuss that issue when we go to sign the papers. Maybe we'll eat in the *cantina*."

"Not unless you wanna die of some sort of poisoning," Clay said with a laugh.

"Poisoning?" Teresa said. "Why? What's wrong? Juan is a good cook."

"I guess he forgot to tell you," Jose said with a chuckle. "Juan quit and now works for a large restaurant in San Antonio. The owner of the *cantina* was trying to cook when we were there, and I don't think he's any good at it."

"*Santa Maria*," Teresa said, crossing her breast in the sign of a cross. "Those poor people."

"Well, ya need to be prepared for ol' Charlie to ask you to go to work for him running the kitchen. I told him no, that we have a baby now and a ranch to run, but I don't think he'll listen to me."

"Maybe he should ask Rob to run the kitchen while he looks for someone to replace Juan," Teresa said thoughtfully as they approached the buggy.

"Ain't a half-bad idea," Clay said with a snicker. "From what I see, Clara Jean hates being on the ranch. Maybe she'll like living in town."

"Maybe," Teresa said as Clay helped her into the buggy. "Sometimes she acts happy and like she's my best friend. Other times she hates me. I think she's loco."

"Maybe she's with child," Jose said as he helped Juanita into the other side of the buggy. He laughed as Clay and Teresa stared at him.

"Juanita acted much the same way while she was pregnant. Maybe … ?"

"I did not,"Juanita snapped.

"*Mi bella esposa*," Jose said as he leaned in the buggy and kissed her. "There were times I was happy to lead the regiment out to chase *banditos*."

"Ah, you should ask the Holy Mother to pray for you. Lying is still a sin." Juanita tilted her head up and glared into the distance.

"So is pride." He tried kissing her again but her face became a moving target.

Clay laughed loudly as he mounted Loco.

"Well, y'all can always scratch one another's eyes out later. Let's head to town and buy a ranch. Maybe Maria will feed us. She cooks almost as good as Teresa." He cocked his head and grinned at Teresa.

"Not as good, mind you, but pretty good."

"*Bueno*," Teresa said with a giggle. "That was good, *marido muy fuerte*." She nodded and took the reins, "That was good." She started the buggy forward.

Chapter 32

The *cantina* was busy when Clay and Jose entered. Charlie was behind the counter serving beer and shots of whiskey to dusty cowpunchers, while a young Mexican filled two mugs with beer for Henry Jenkins and Roy Johnson.

"How come you're not wearing a star?" Clay asked as he elbowed in next to Roy.

"No need to," Roy said and took a sip. "Ray says he's almost back to normal. He's been toting his iron and making the rounds the past couple of days. Town's pretty quiet anyway."

"Huh, I figured Maria would've put a leash on him."

"She tried, but he wasn't having any of it." Ray took another sip. "They're still barking at each other some, but she's not changing him."

"Maybe we should listen to our women," Jose said "Juanita never liked it when I went on patrol. She said it was dangerous." He raised his eyebrows and cocked his head. "It was."

Jose raised two fingers as Charlie approached. "Dos *tequilas, por favor.*"

"And a bucket of beer to go," Clay added.

Charlie poured the tequilas first, then started filling the tin bucket with draft beer.

"Still ain't found a cook?"

"Nah, thought I was gonna get Tomás, but Lucia pitched a fit. She said she wasn't having him working 'round here and leaving her home alone with six kids."

"Well, he makes a good living building and repairing things for folks as it is, and he spends most of his time right at home. Got anyone else in mind?" Clay sipped the tequila.

"No, I'm about to give up and sell most of those pots and pans … maybe even the stove. I could use the room for storage anyway."

Charlie set the bucket of beer on the counter and Clay laid down a gold coin.

"Well, before you do, I might have someone in mind," Clay said as Charlie fetched his change.

"Yeah? Who?"

"You remember Rob Mayfield?"

"That young sodbuster who came in the day Teresa had her baby?"

"Yeah."

"What about him? Can he cook?"

"Teresa taught him."

"*Sí*," Jose said with a nod. "He cooks for all those living at Clay's ranch. It would be a shame to lose him. He cooks very well."

"Well, send him my way."

"He's got a wife and baby," Clay said. "He ain't gonna work for less than top dollar."

"*Sí*, and he's a friend of Teresa's," Jose said with a grin. "She might get angry if she thought you were not being honest with him." He shook his head and finished his tequila. "I wouldn't want her angry with me."

"No sir." Clay finished his glass and rapped it against the bar. "Believe me, she ain't too fun to be around when she's peeved. But I'll tell him to look you up."

******

"That's not true." Teresa creased her forehead as Clay chuckled. He had just told her about his conversation with Charlie at the *cantina*, with a few embellishments from Jose thrown in. "People like being around me, even when I'm angry."

"Think so? How 'bout Hugh Tullis, the former owner of the *cantina*?" Ray asked. "Seems I remember a time you were fixin' to open the top of his head with one of your pearl-handled .38's."

Teresa came from where she had been helping Maria in the kitchen to yell in Ray's face.

"He was not a nice man. He …. he …"

"I know what he did to you," Ray said. "And I was sort of hoping to hang the son-of-a-bitch, but his brother-in-law splattered his brains all over my jail instead."

"Couldn't happen to a nicer guy," Clay said as he filled six glasses with beer. "I was gonna beat the stuffings outa him until you stopped me." He handed one of the glasses to Ray.

"I thought you did." Ray toasted Clay with the glass. "He was half dead when I locked him up."

"Let's change the subject," Maria said, setting a plate full of tortillas on the table. "Get your sons. The food is ready."

"Whoa, Hoss," Clay said, grabbing one of the twins as he ran by. "You can sit on Uncle Clay's lap while we eat some grub, if you want."

They crowded around the table as best they could and Ray said the blessing.

"Everyone, help yourselves," Maria said, and Clay began filling his plate with rice, beans and spicy chicken.

"So, you gonna tell Rob that Charlie wants to talk turkey with him?" Clay said over a mouthful.

"*Sí*, I can if you think he'll want the job," Teresa said with a nod.

"He should at least have the chance to refuse, either way. I don't figure Clara Jean likes being way out there where there's nobody for miles."

"She's young," Juanita said quietly. "She'll change as she gets older." She shrugged and spooned some beans and rice onto a tortilla. "I personally like the quiet. Coming to town to buy canned goods once every two weeks or so is fine with me."

"Amen, sister," Clay said, toasting her with a tortilla. "Cows seldom argue and cause you trouble."

"They don't shoot you either," Maria said.

"Point taken," Ray said, creasing his brow. He laid his fork in his plate.

"My wife wants me to give up being a lawman. But it's all I've ever done. You can understand what I'm saying, Clay."

"Sure I understand, but an old dog can still learn new tricks," Clay said with a grin. "Look at me. I know a whole lot more about being a lawman than I do running a ranch, but I'm learning. And I think we'll make it, in spite of me."

"Maybe, but I ain't got the money you have, either."

"Well ... maybe we can cure that."

Everyone grew quiet and glanced at each other.

"I ain't talked it over with Teresa, but it's about time to collect the rest of that gold. You and Jose are welcome to join in, if it's okay with you, Teresa."

"*Sí*, when do we go?" Teresa said.

"*We* don't go. *I* go. You stay home with little Yolanda."

"Ah!" she almost yelled. "That is *my* gold. I was married to Refugio when he hid it, not you!"

"True, but Yolanda's gonna need raising, and I don't want to make her an orphan. If something went wrong, and I didn't make it back, she'll need you to take care of her."

"Actually, the gold belongs to the Mexican government. It is stolen payroll," Jose said with a grin.

"You aiming to give your cut back to them?" Clay asked.

"No," Jose said with a chuckle. "I would like to use my ... cut, as you say, to bring our son and his family to the ranch and take care of our grandchildren. I'm just saying the Federales might take a different view if we're caught, and they are very proficient with a firing squad."

"Well, that's why I want you and Ray along. It might also be good to take Julio along. He's good tracking and handles a gun like he was born with one. So," he held his glass of beer high, "how about it? Y'all in?"

Ray and Jose both looked at their wives, and only raised their glasses when all three women raised theirs in unison.

"We go right after this Westfall thing gets settled."

"That's a skunk with a different odor," Ray said. "No one's heard hide nor hair of him lately. They figure it might've been him that gunned down everyone on that Wells Fargo stage a little over a week ago, but they're not sure, and no one knows where they went."

"Well, I kind of figure they're just laying low and spending the money they took. I know Westfall enough to know he's gonna come gunning for me sooner or later. He's got a score to settle; he'll crawl out of the woodwork pretty soon. I'd feel better surprising him, and getting this settled before he gets anywhere near Cool Water, or Carrizo Springs for that matter."

Chapter 33

"Let's see ..." Clay stared at Clara Jean who was seated on the weathered bench in front of the Cool Water Saloon. The hem of her skirt had been hiked just above the top of her laced work boot, revealing a shapely stockinged ankle.

"Here, he said passing the small holster to Rob. "She's your wife. You strap it on her."

Rob took the holster and knelt in front of Clara. He attempted to place it several different ways before staring at Clay helplessly.

"How?"

"Well, if it was me, and I was wearing one, I'd want it with the pistol on the outside of my leg, like this." Clay held the holster to his ankle. "That way, if I needed it, I could just do this." He hiked his right leg quickly and pretended to draw the small .25 caliber pistol.

"Hmm," Rob said with a nod. "That makes sense."

Clara walked back and forth in front of the saloon, holding the hem of her skirt above the holster, staring at the extra leather.

"Now, try it with the gun," Clay said, handing the pistol to Rob.

Clara paced back and forth again, studying the weapon with each step. A small audience had gathered to see what was happening.

"Are you sure it's wise to have it way down there, beneath her dress?" Theodore asked.

"And where else should she have it?" Hildegarde said. "She can't wear it like Clay or Julio, on her hip."

"Why not?"

"Because it'll get in her way, carrying our grandson or doing chores."

"Well, I asked Hans, and he said a lot of women in the large cities are wearing ankle pistols, and it's also caught on with some men," Clay said as he walked around Clara in a slow circle.

"I don't know why an *hombre* would use one of those," Leo Santiago said with a snicker.

"I think he means the rich men who wear ..." Rebecca Santiago motioned with her hands, trying to find the right word in English.

"Suit?" Hildegarde said.

"*Sí*, suit," Rebecca said with a smile.

"You speak English very well, dear," Hildegarde said, bringing an even bigger smile from her.

"Well, let's go see if you know how to shoot the thing," Clay said.

Clara handed William to his grandmother and followed Clay past the cemetery and away from the buildings. Everyone followed at a safe distance. Clay stopped about a dozen yards from a clump of cactus.

"Okay, let's see how hard it is for you to pull the piece."

Clara stared blankly.

"Pull the gun from the holster," he explained.

"Oh." Clara hiked her knee and retrieving the pistol with ease.

"Good, good," Clay said with a nod. "A little slow, but with some practice, I think you'll do okay. Now, load it," he said, handing her a box of ammunition.

"Me?"

"Yes, you. You're not always going to have me or your father and husband around. You're going to have to clean and load the gun yourself, and now's the time to learn."

Clara took her time filling the cylinder with bullets and snapping it closed.

"Okay, now show me how you shot that Indian."

Clay cringed as Clara pointed the pistol toward the cactus and closed her eyes before pulling the trigger. The gun made a loud pop and she opened her eyes as the bullet ricocheted off a rock with a whine.

"Not bad, if you don't wanna shoot anything."

"I missed?"

"Completely," Clay said with a chuckle. "Now, you want to show me how you shot the Indian?"

"I don't know it just happened," Clara said, staring at the pistol.

"You pa didn't teach you how to handle a gun?" Clay scrunched his eyebrows.

"Well, yeah ... he showed me how to shoot our shotgun. I can handle one pretty good. Want me to show you?"

"No," Clay shook his head, "I doubt you're gonna be lugging a twelve gauge around everywhere you go."

He heaved a sigh and stood behind her with his hands on her shoulders. He lowered his head to speak directly in her ear and yelled.

"It's an Apache, and he's got your baby! He's taking William! Now, Clara, now!"

Clara screamed and fired twice, hitting the cactus with both shots.

"There you are. That was good, very good."

"That was a mean trick, Mr. Best," Clara said with a scowl.

"Maybe, but it proved one thing."

"And what's that?"

"It proved you're a mama bear willing to fight for your cub. Look," he added as she continued glaring. "There ain't but one reason for pulling that gun. You only pull it to shoot. And the only reason to point it at another human, no matter if he's a renegade warrior, or a thieving scoundrel in town, and that is to shoot them."

"But I don't wanna shoot anyone, Mr. Best."

"None of us do, honey," Clay said. "Only a crazy man will kill when there's no need in killing. But there's some real bad people out there, so you'd better learn how to shoot that thing, and learn to shoot it good."

He dropped the box of ammunition in her hand.

"I want you to empty that box into that clump of cactus. Start by picking a spot and trying to hit the same spot with every shot."

"Where do you want me to stand?"

"Right here. Don't move. And when you've run out of ammunition, come look me up at the house and I'll teach you how to clean and oil it."

Clay turned away and looked back over his shoulder.

"We'll do it again tomorrow and the day after that, until I figure you can handle it without hurting yourself or one of us."

Chapter 34

James rose early and got dressed. He was pulling on his last boot when Edita stirred with a deep moan. She propped herself on one elbow and smiled at him.

"Where you go so early, *mi amor*?"

"Well, I'll tell you where I'm going Edita. My funds are gettin' kinda low, so I figure it's about time to go back to work."

"Oh, no, you're not going to leave me again," she said with her bottom lip poked out.

"Yeah, we've been here most of the month," James said with a grin. "I thought you'd be getting tired of me about now."

"Oh, no," she said, crawling out of the bed and perching her naked body in his lap. "I never get tired of my Jimmy-boy."

"I reckon you'd get tired of me real quick if I ran out of money."

"Never." She kissed him with a pouty mouth. "I'll never get tired of Jimmy. Here," she held his hand against one of her breasts. "Feel my heart, it's broken for you."

"Well, I'll just have to fix it."

James carried her to the bed and removed his boots. It wouldn't matter much if they got a late start. There was always another stage or bank waiting to be robbed, and he knew where Clay Best would most likely be. He swore by all the devils in hell he was going to find Clay and settle the score this time, or die trying.

******

James stopped in the shade of an outcropping of rocks and mopped the sweat from his face with a neckerchief. He found himself wishing he had turned Edita's offer down and left early. While he always found the whore pleasurable in bed, the Texas heat was unbearable.

"Hell, I thought it was supposed to be fall," Curley said, taking a sip from his canteen.

"It *is* fall. It just don't know it yet."

James dismounted and loosened the cinches on his saddle.

"Whadda ya think, Carlos? Should we make camp right here, or do you know a better spot somewhere close?"

"Here is good," Carlos said and dismounted. The *vaquero* hadn't said a dozen words since they left, and James figured he must've fallen in love with that skinny whore he'd been staying with. The sad part was, the kid was too stupid to know she would run him off the minute he ran out of money, the same as any whore would.

James tossed his saddle into the shade of the rocks as his horse took a roll in the sand. If Carlos didn't get his mind out of the whore's bed and back on the job ahead, he'd have to replace him. Thinking of the woman while robbing a stage would get you killed.

******

James checked his nickel-plated pocket watch. It was approximately ten o'clock and the heat was starting to bear down like a blast furnace, adding to his already cranky mood. James never minded having to camp out, especially if it was a nice shady spot with grass and a creek or river close by. But a dry camp where the sand they slept on was as hot as a frying pan had left something to be desired.

"Hey, Carlos," he yelled to the *vaquero* perched on the rocks with the spyglass. "See anything yet?"

"*Sí*. A cloud of dust coming our way. Horses, I think."

"Yeah, the stage," James said with a chuckle. "How far?"

"Um, five miles, maybe."

"Get down here and get ready! Let's see what they're carrying and get out of this burning hell."

Carlos descended in a slide of rock and dust as James and Curley tossed their saddles on the horses. The dust cloud had grown considerably larger by the time the horses were ready. James pulled his rifle from the scabbard and looked at his trusted companions.

"Just like last time. Carlos, you slip over to the other side of the road behind them rocks and pick off the guard when they round the bend. I'll get the driver, and Curley, you slow the mules. Now, we've done this before, so they're likely to be looking for something to happen, so be ready for anything.

James found a spot where he could see the stage coming. His rifle was already hot to the touch. Then, suddenly, the rumble of hooves and metal-rimmed wheels reached his ears. The rumble grew louder until he could see the coach through the dust. Then the unexpected happened. Several armed riders mounted on horseback moved from behind the stage to take the lead. James cursed loudly and started to call for a halt when Carlos fired, hitting one of the mounted guards and knocking him from the saddle.

The stage slowed quickly as one of the guards returned fire, kicking up dust near Carlos.

"Dammit to hell," James yelled, and shot the guard. The third guard dismounted and took cover behind some rocks, firing at James. He ducked and ran, trying to skirt the guard and get a better shot. He raised to draw a bead on the man when Carlos fired, hitting the shotgun guard. The guard slumped and the driver dropped to the ground trying to help him down. James chose the driver instead, shooting the man in the back.

The exchange of gunfire lasted for several minutes, and ended with James and Curley killing everyone inside the stage.

"Hey, *Jefe*," Carlos yelled.

"Yeah?"

"This one is still alive." Carlos stood over one of the mounted guards as he writhed with pain.

"Well, kill 'em."

"*Porque*?"

"I said, kill him."

"But, *Jefe*."

"My hell, Mendoza. You were willing to kill the shotgun guard and shoot that sheriff in the back. What's different about this one?" James growled. He walked to where Carlos stood and shot the guard in the head.

"I don't know what's kept you alive this long. Besides," he glared at the stunned *vaquero*. "It'd be worse to leave him laying out here suffering. This way, I stopped him from suffering. Think about that.

"Now, come on. Let's see what's in the strong box and get outa here."

Chapter 35

"Is Captain Ramos around?"

Joseph Lincoln looked even bigger than she had remembered, sitting high on the buckboard. He dwarfed Charlie Roberts who was seated beside him.

"*Sí*," Teresa shaded her eyes against the noonday sun and smiled. "Please get down and come into the *cantina*. We are about ready to eat."

"That was what I was hoping," Charlie jumped down and inhaled deeply, then grinned. "Smells real good."

He started toward the saloon but stopped to look back at her. "I always like to test someone before I offer them a job."

"*Sí*, I suppose you are thinking of offering Rob a job at your *cantina*?"

"Yes, but only if he can cook."

Teresa took Joseph by the arm as they headed toward the saloon.

"Ain't no way for him to hide what he's interested in," Joseph said with a chuckle. "Half the folks that used to hang out in his saloon quit coming since he lost Juan."

"Really? I thought they went there to get drunk."

"I reckon some of them did, and they still come ... mostly. But a good number came to eat and drink a cold beer. Problem is, the restaurant started selling beer last week, and that's hit his business pretty hard."

"I see. Then he needs someone who cooks better food than the restaurant, doesn't he?"

"I suppose so. Where did you say Captain Ramos is?"

"He is inside the *cantina*, waiting to eat. What do you need him for?"

"He asked me to check his wagon out. Says he wants to take a trip, and he doesn't want it to break down."

"Ah, yes," Teresa nodded as they reached the saloon. "He did mention taking a trip to see his son." She paused at the door.

"I shall be sorry to see Rob go, if he accepts *Señor* Roberts' offer. It will mean I'll have to start cooking once again."

"Maybe I should stay out here, ma'am."

¿"Porque?"

"Well, you see, some folks don't want to eat or drink with a black man."

Teresa tilted her head and laughed loudly.

"Come, *Señor* Lincoln. In here, you will be eating with Mexicans and Indians. Unless, you don't choose to eat with Mexicans and Indians."

Joseph chuckled and shook his head.

"No, ma'am. I gots no qualms about eating with other folks."

Charlie had already seated himself at a table next to Clara Jean and her parents. Teresa sat next to Clay at the next table and patted the empty chair next to her.

"Sit here, *Señor* Lincoln. The girls will serve you."

One of the Indian girls was already making her way among the tables, stopping at each chair and dishing steaming rice onto the plates. She was followed by another girl carrying a plate of hot tortillas. Isabel entered the back door carrying a large bowl of steaming pinto beans, stewed with onion, garlic and bacon. The dish was seasoned with chili peppers, cilantro and sausage. Isabel smiled as she dumped a heaping spoonful over the rice. Charlie took a bite and closed his eyes as he savored the flavor.

"Oh, my Lord," he said after swallowing. "I've eaten a lot of beans and rice in my time, but nothing as good as this."

"It's called *habas del vaquero*, or cowboy beans," Teresa said with a grin. "I think it would be something the people at your *cantina* would enjoy eating."

"You've got that right." Charlie tore off a chunk of tortilla and filled it with the rice and beans.

"*Sí*, it is too bad *Señor* Rob works here and not at your *cantina*. The people would enjoy his cooking, the same as we do every day." Teresa grinned and took a sip of wine.

"Well, I aim to cure that, right away," Charlie said over a mouthful.

"Oh, I did not know he was considering such a thing. No one has discussed it with me, and I am the one who taught him to cook and trained him. Have you asked him, yet?"

"Not yet, ma'am, but I aim to, right after I've finished eating."

"Oh," Teresa said with a nod. "And what if he does not agree to leave. I think he and his family like staying here at Cool Water."

Clara Jean started to speak, but her mother silenced her by grabbing her arm and shaking her head.

"It is a beautiful ranch and we have offered them employment and are willing to make them partners." She shook her head slowly. "It would be a lot to give up to live in town and do what? Cook for the drunks inside your *cantina*. What would he get out of that, *señor*? He has a beautiful wife and son to think of. What could you offer them to make up the loss?"

Charlie chewed slowly as he stared at her. He swallowed and took a sip of wine.

"Ma'am, you don't mean to keep him here, do you?"

"And why not? *Señor* Rob and I have been friends for a long time. Why shouldn't I want to keep him here?"

"But ma'am. I'm in need of a cook real bad. Not having one is hurting my business something fierce."

Teresa scooted her chair around to face him.

"Okay, tell me, *señor*, what have you to offer that I cannot give better?"

"Aw, hell!" Charlie glanced toward Clay. "What's going on here. I thought you said he was willing to come work for me, Clay."

"No sir, I didn't say such a thing." Clay shook his head. "What I said was, that Rob was a pretty darned good cook, and that Teresa had taught him. I also said, I didn't think Clara Jean liked living here much, but come to think of it, I ain't heard nothing bad or negative coming outa her in quite a while, so maybe she's changed her tune some. I think what Teresa's asking is reasonable. What *are* you willing to offer?"

Charlie heaved a sigh and ran a hand across his face.

"I'll pay top wages. I'll give him Sundays off. I've been thinking of shutting the saloon Sundays anyways. They can live in town and get the boy educated in the school when he's old enough."

"We are going to build a school also to teach all the children living here," Teresa said with a shrug. "Rob will be giving up his ownership of his portion of the ranch if he leaves. Are you willing to give him part of your *cantina* in return?"

Clara's mouth dropped open as she stared at Teresa wide-eyed.

"My hell, woman! Are you trying to hold me up?"

"No, I am simply asking if you're going to take care of my friend or not?"

Charlie pointed a finger and Clay. "You had something to do with this, didn't you?"

"No sir. Teresa's always had a mind of her own."

"All right!" Charlie slapped his palm against the table. "I'll make him part owner, but I'll be damned if I'm going to let him run the place!"

"I don't think he would, *Señor* Charlie," Teresa said with a grin. "All he will want to run is the kitchen. You will be in charge of the rest. He will get forty-percent of the profit from the kitchen, and you will buy all the supplies. And," she turned her chair back around and grinned at Clara, "I will check once in a while to see if you are taking care of my friends."

Clay raised his eyebrows and cocked his head to one side.

"Sounds reasonable to me, Charlie. Whadda you say?"

Charlie took a sip of wine and glared at the back of Teresa's head.

"I think I've just been hornswoggled, that's what I think."

Chapter 36

"We've kinda got a problem," Curley said, taking a swig from his canteen. He had spent the last two days watching the movements of Clay and Teresa Best as he remained hidden.

"Why, what's the problem? It shouldn't be too hard figuring his movements." James frowned and took a sip from the bottle of whiskey he'd been nursing the past hour.

"The problem is, the place is crawling with Mexicans and Indians."

"Indians?"

"Yeah, and not just any Indians. Carlos figures they're Yaqui, and that's a handful." Curley sat beside James in the shade of a mesquite and began rolling a cigarette. "I left Carlos there to watch."

"What about Clay? You had to see him once or twice."

"Sure, I've seen him. But he's always surrounded by a bunch of them Mexicans, like Leo Santiago and Julio Garcia, and they've usually got some of those Yaqui or that big farmer or Mexican captain with 'em. It ain't that easy to get close to Clay without getting yourself shot to hell."

"Hell, guess I've got to do everything myself."

James took a long pull on the bottle and struggled to his feet. Curley shook his head as James staggered a few feet to relieve himself on some rocks. There were several empty whiskey bottles scattered around the campsite, and Curley figured that's what James had been living on the past two days.

"And what would you have done differently?" Curley snapped as James staggered back to plop back into the shade.

"I'd have waited until he was alone and snatched him and brought him back here like I said."

"That's what we'd planned to do, boss, but like I said, it ain't that easy. He's never alone."

"Hell, you idgit! He's got to take a crap or a piss once in a while, don't he? And I don't figure he's goanna take a bunch of Indians or Mexicans into the outhouse with him, is he?"

Curley studied James thoughtfully for a second before chuckling. "No, I don't reckon he is, especially in the middle of the night." He stood and stretched his stocky frame. "Reckon I'll mosey back to where I left Carlos and see if we can't take care of that tonight. Got any more of those canned beans? We ran out of grub this morning."

"Yeah, over in the pack. Help yourself."

Curley removed four cans from the pack and stuffed them into his saddlebags. "See you tonight."

He swung into the saddle and trotted the sweaty horse toward Cool Water, wondering why he hadn't thought to watch the outhouse. It should be even easier than if he had tried grabbing Clay in daylight, since few people took a gun into the outhouse in the middle of the night. Curley chuckled. Maybe that was why James was the leader and he wasn't. He simply didn't think of small details like that.

It would be easier, in Curley's mind, to simply put a bullet in the ex-lawman, but James was insisting on taking him alive. He wanted to teach him a lesson and make him suffer for the trouble he'd caused; beat the hell out of him first, then kill him. That was a real worry in the back of Curley's mind. He'd watched Clay give James a first-class whipping in the Cool Water Saloon, and taking Clay Best alive wasn't going to be an easy task for anyone. It just might be something that would get them all killed.

Chapter 37

"*Carumba*," Carlos said in a hoarse whisper. "Don't they ever sleep?"

"Guess not. You'd best get some shut-eye. I'll keep watch."

"*Bueno.*"

Carlos slumped back and closed his eyes, pulling a dirty saddle blanket across his body. Curley cupped his hand to light a smoke, then made himself as comfortable as possible. Cool Water was mostly dark, with only two windows showing the glow of yellow lamplight. A campfire smoldered in the middle of the Yaqui camp, with a few Indians still milling around. Curley figured they must be women, taking care of a few minor details before calling it a night.

He'd recognized Clay's hulking frame a few times as he wandered from the saloon to the outhouse, and back to his own house; then, once again when the young man who had been cooking earlier knocked on his door. They had really taken a chance coming this close to Cool Water. Curley figured all the cards had been dealt around mid-afternoon when several Yaqui chased a steer within yards of where they were hiding. The only thing that had saved them from being discovered was when the steer turned and headed in the opposite direction.

He slapped a mosquito against his cheek, then scratched a spot on his arm. He was sure he'd been bitten by sand fleas a million times. James was gonna owe him big time when this thing was over. Sticking up a small bank or stage was one thing --- that helped put money in everyone's pocket --- but this thing with Clay Best was simply personal between Jim and Clay. Curley didn't figure it would benefit him or Carlos one little bit, and he didn't carry any grudge toward Cay of any kind.

Curley had thought back several times about the beating James had taken, and figured he had deserved the whipping. But James had always been a little crazy when he drank, and they had really been pouring down the whisky with Les Bishop when Clay entered the saloon right after discovering his wife had died. It didn't take long before James said something stupid about her being a lunger, and was better off dead. He had always wondered what had kept him from blowing James' brains all over the saloon. Instead he chose to give him one hell of a beating. He might've beaten him to death, if those two cowboys had not dragged him from the saloon. He would've deserved it either way. Curley had drunk his share of rotgut, but he couldn't remember saying anything that stupid ... ever.

He rolled and smoked half a dozen cigarettes and watched the lighted windows go dark. The Indian campfire died to a glow after the women disappeared. It was about midnight when Clay came from the house, wearing pants and boots with long johns covering his chest. Curley didn't see any gun belt.

"Carlos," he whispered, nudging the *vaquero* with his boot.

"*Sí.*" He sat up quickly, rubbing his eyes.

"He's headed toward the outhouse. Come on."

Curley grabbed the coiled rope and lead the way. They ran past the back of the saloon and across the road to flank the outhouse from both sides. They had barely reached the weathered building when Clay came out, buttoning his trousers. Without slowing his momentum, Curley crashed the butt of his .45 against Clay's skull. The big man fell with a grunt.

"Grab his feet," Curley whispered. It took about two minutes to carry the heavy frame back to the waiting horses and throw him across the packhorse. It felt like an eternity.

"Tie him good," he said as Carlos wrapped the rope around Clay's hands and feet. "I don't wanna go through this again."

Chapter 38

Teresa woke with the sound of Yolanda's crying. The empty spot beside her where Clay slept didn't alarm her, since he was normally up much earlier and making coffee. She padded in her bare feet to the cradle and picked up her fussing baby.

"*Carumba*! You are a wet one and hungry, aren't you, *chica*?"

She changed the wet diaper, then crawled back in bed to feed Yolanda. When she was full, Teresa covered herself and burped her.

Isabel woke with a yawn and smiled at her from across the room.

"*Buenos dias, Doña* Teresa. "*¿Cómo estás hoy?*"

"I am doing well this morning. And how are you?"

"Very well. Where is *Señor* Clay?"

"He wakes early, so he's probably outside visiting the men. But," she crossed the room toward Isabel, "he should bring me coffee before talking to a bunch of men. I will bite his ear off for doing such a thing."

Isabel giggled as Teresa handed Yolanda to her.

"Here, watch her while I visit the *letrina, por favor.*"

Isabel smiled and cooed softly at the baby as Teresa hurried out the door. She exited the outhouse a few minutes later and bumped into Captain Ramos who was waiting his turn.

"*Buenos dias, señora*. Where is that husband of yours? Sleeping late?"

"No, I assumed he was drinking coffee and visiting with you men."

"No, I haven't seen him."

"You haven't?"

"No, but I slept later than I should."

He slipped past her and opened the outhouse door, then looked back.

"I will find him in a few moments and tell him that you are looking for him."

Teresa ambled slowly back toward her house, hoping to see Clay laughing and talking with someone, but there was no sign of him. She entered the house. Pedro and Leticia Diego were both awake and crowded close to Isabel, watching Yolanda. She quickly dressed before taking Yolanda and smiling at them.

"Isabel, I need you to do me a favor, *por favor*."

"*¿Sí?*"

"I need you to take care of Pedro and Leticia, while I find my husband."

"Is something wrong, *Doña* Teresa?"

"No ... I don't believe there is. But, it's not like him to fix coffee and forget to bring me a cup before doing what he has planned. Captain Ramos hasn't seen him either, so something must have gone wrong somewhere. Maybe at the Yaqui camp. So, will you fix them something to eat and watch them for me?"

" *Sí, Doña* Teresa, I will be happy to watch them for you."

Teresa slipped Yolanda into her sling and making sure the baby's eyes would be shaded, stepped into the morning sun. She shook her head, thinking of the several times she had corrected Isabel about calling her *Doña* Teresa. The girl insisted that she must be a *Doña*, since they owned such a large rancho and took care of all the people living there. She finally decided to let her have her way, since it wouldn't matter either way.

She approached Rob and Clara as they were coming from the saloon.

"We were coming to see you, ma'am," Clara said with a warm smile.

"Oh?"

"Yes, we're thinking of taking Mr. Roberts up on his offer and move to Carrizo Springs. That is, if it wouldn't cause any problems for you."

Teresa pursed her lips thoughtfully for a second before smiling.

"No, I think it would be a good thing for you. But," she held her index finger in the air, "expect me to check once in a while to make sure he is treating you well. You may live in the *jacale* until you find a place of your own."

Rob smiled and gently squeezed her hand.

"I might be asking your advice every now and then about cooking."

"That would be fine, but I think you will be creating your own dishes soon. Now, I must find my husband. Have you seen him?"

"No, I haven't. I'll tell him you're looking for him if I see him."

"*Gracias.*"

Teresa turned away and Clara joined her, stride by stride, bouncing William in her arms. Teresa glanced at her and Clara smiled.

"I thought I'd join you. You don't mind, do you?"

"No," Teresa shook her head. "Maybe four eyes will help me find my husband better. What is it you want?"

"Mainly, some female company." Clara giggled. "I love Rob terribly, but between him and my brother and father, I get tired of listening to them. Then, you throw in the rest of the men ... I need some female company."

"What about your mother? Doesn't she talk to you?"

"Yes, but it's not the same. She's my mother. I tried talking to Rebecca and Estrella, but they don't know English very well."

"Maybe you should learn Spanish." Teresa stopped at the edge of the Yaqui village and studied the milling Indians preparing for the day. "And what about *Señora* Ramos? She speaks excellent English."

"Yes, she does. And I do talk to her once in a while, but ... it's just that you're ... so ..." She shrugged.

Teresa turned to stare at her.

"I'm so what, *señora*? I know you do not like me very well, but that's okay. You married my friend, and he loves you very much, so I have chosen to like you regardless."

"Oh, no." Clara grabbed her arm. "I do like you, a whole lot. It's just that you're so pretty, and you can do everything. And I thought you and Rob had been more than friends, so I was jealous. I will admit that. But what I want now is to be like you. It's like you can do anything."

Teresa tilted her head back and laughed.

"*Chica*, just be yourself. You'll be fine. Now, please help me find my Clay. No one has seen him."

"Is something wrong?"

"I don't know, but this is not like him. He always tells me where he is going."

"Okay, I'll help."

Teresa grinned as the girl dashed toward her parent's wagon. In a matter of minutes a full-scale search was taking place. It was approximately a half-hour later when Captain Ramos joined her at the corral.

"I am sorry, *señora*, we have looked everywhere. We can't seem to find *Señor* Clay. You don't suppose he left early for Carrizo Springs? I know he was thinking of seeing Sheriff King."

Teresa slowly shook her head.

"No, *Capitán*, he would never go without telling me, or leave without Loco." She pointed toward the black stallion. "I'm really worried, *Capitan*, this is not like Clay. Something has happened to him."

" *Señora*!" Leo yelled as he ran toward them. "The Yaqui called El Pájaro Correr has found something. Come, I'll show you."

Teresa walked briskly toward the outhouse where a small crowd had gathered. She had spoken to the tall Yaqui known as El Pájaro Correr only once; he was a pleasant young man who seldom spoke, unless he had something worth saying. His name literally meant Running Bird, making her believe he had been named after the running birds that frequented that part of Texas. Leo and Theodore were trying desperately to keep the crowd corralled in front of the privy.

"What is it?" Teresa asked as Yolanda woke and started to cry.

"There has been a struggle," Leo said excitedly. "See where somebody was dragged behind the building, then carried away."

Teresa followed the faint marks left in the dirt by a pair of boot heels. She gazed toward the north where a group of Indians were following a set of tracks.

"Where is Running Bird?"

"I reckon he's the one in the lead, over there, ma'am." Theodore pointed toward several Indians following a trail.

"Please tell him I would like to speak to him."

Rob took off in a run without saying a word. Teresa walked a ways toward them, then stopped as Rob and the Indian approached.

"Please tell me what you think happened."

Running Bird stared blankly for a couple of seconds before looking at Estrella who had joined Teresa's side.

"He says that someone dragged another man and then carried him over there." Estrella pointed toward the Yaquis following the tracks. "The man was then put on a horse and taken away."

"Was he hurt?"

Estrella interpreted the question in a mixture of Spanish and Yaqui, then nodded at the reply.

"He says yes, he found some blood, but only a little. He also says they were trying to hide their trail by wrapping rags around the horses' feet."

"*Gracias*. Tell him I am in his debt, and I have one more question. Ask him if he can follow the tracks. I want to bring my husband back home where he belongs."

The Yaqui quickly nodded.

"*Gracias*. Tell him I'll be ready quickly."

She turned to survey the crowd.

"Leo, Julio, Captain Ramos and *Señor* Russell, saddle the horses and arm yourselves, and take an extra horse for *Señor* Clay. We will get my husband and punish those that took him. The rest of you will stay here and protect the children and yourselves."

She then placed a gentle hand on Clara's shoulder.

"*Señora,* you wanted to help. Take care of my Yolanda for me."

"I will, and don't worry about a thing." Clara matched Teresa's stride as they headed toward the house.

"I fed her this morning, but she may get hungry and fussy. I am sorry to ask, but I must find out what happened to my Clay."

Clara smiled as she took Yolanda and sat on the edge of the bed. "That is not a problem. I have enough milk for both babies. You go do what you have to do. We'll be fine."

"*Gracias*," Teresa kissed her cheek, "you and I will be strong women together."

"I hope so. Just be careful. I'd hate to lose you."

"Pray and we will be fine."

Chapter 39

Clay woke with a buffalo-sized headache. It took a few minutes for him to realize that everything ached, and even longer to find he was laid cross-ways across a saddle with a rope around his wrists and feet.

James Westfall!

The thought angered him more than frightened him. He knew there wasn't much he could do to defend himself, especially tied to a horse. Besides, he didn't have a gun, and didn't know if he could focus enough to put up much of a fight. The horses stopped moving and the riders dismounted. He recognized Westfall's voice as he joined them.

"I'll be damned, you got him!"

"That we did." Curley cut the rope and let Clay fall to the ground with a thud.

"Why's he all bloody?"

"I had to give him a little bonk on the noodle to keep him quiet. Didn't feel like having to shoot my way out of Cool Water, especially with Julio Garcia and Leo Santiago there."

James kicked Clay in the ribs and got no response.

"He ain't dead is he?"

"I don't think so." Curley slapped Clay across the face without a response. "Hell, I didn't think I hit him that hard."

"You sonofabitch." James hit Curley in the jaw, knocking him to the ground. "I wanted him alive, not dead."

"He lives," Carlos said.

"What?"

"He lives. The heart beats," he said with his ear against Clay's chest. "But he doesn't wake."

"He's in ... what'd they call it when Rio fell off his horse and landed on his head?"

"Coma was what I remember," James said.

"Yeah, coma. That means he don't hear of feel anything."

"Well, it ain't what I wanted. I wanted to beat the hell out of him, then kill him real slow to make up for all the trouble he's caused."

"You can still do that, *Jefe*," Carlos said.

"What fun is there in that, if he can't feel it?" James kicked Clay hard. "Na, I wanted him to feel every blow, like he done to me that day in the Cool Water Saloon."

"So, what are we going to do? Want me to plug him for you?" Curley pulled his .45.

"Na, killing him outright would just put him outa his misery. I've been thinking it over while you was gone. Drag him over between those mesquites. We're gonna stretch him out and let the sun turn him into jerky. Who knows? Maybe he'll wake up and feel it some."

"Maybe the coyotes will eat him," Carlos said as he tied a rope around Clay's wrists, then fed it around a thick branch in a dead mesquite.

"Yeah, maybe," James laughed. "That'd be rich. Pull 'em tight. I don't want him to wake and somehow wiggle out of them ropes."

Chapter 40

Clay woke with the sun glaring in his face. His head still throbbed and his throat was dry as bleached bones.

"Oh, Lord," he croaked. "I got myself into a good fix this time, like a danged idgit."

He tried moving his arms and legs, but they were unmovable. It took a few seconds for him to realize he was tied to the mesquites. He had no idea how long he had been tied, or what time of day it was, but his face felt sunburnt. The sand was already feeling hot against his back. It was going to be another hot one. To make things worse, his ribcage burned with every breath.

"Oh, God, I think they broke several ribs."

He grimaced as he took a deep breath and pulled against the ropes. He gave up with a cry of pain.

"Okay, Lord. I know we ain't always been on the best of speaking terms, but if there's any love at all left for me, help me outa this here fix."

He rolled his head to one side, then back to the other. He'd been left alone to die and become buzzard bait. He'd always figured Westfall would stick around and watch a man suffer. The only reason he could figure they might've rode off was they were afraid of getting caught. It didn't matter much, since it would only take a few hours for a man to shrivel and die in this sun. The first thing to go would be his mind ... he'd go completely mad. Then he'd pass out with a sunstroke and die. He'd heard of folks stranded on the deserts of Arizona and California without water, losing half their body weight through dehydration. He figured it wouldn't be much different for him, if he didn't somehow get out of the ropes.

"Okay, God. I ain't asked for much in my life, and didn't expect much. But I'm asking now for you to help me so I can go home and take care of my wife and daughter."

He slowly inhaled a deep breath, then yelled as he pulled against the ropes. He quit with several painful gasps. The ropes held fast.

"Oh, God ... oh, God. That hurts."

He took another breath and screamed as he jerked violently against the ropes. The dead mesquite gave away with a snap, almost hitting him in the head. He lay painting for a minute, then laughed.

"It weren't exactly what I wanted, but I thank you just the same. Couldn't of done it without you, Lord."

He tugged on the knot with his teeth, and could taste blood by the time the rope fell away. He touched his parched lips with his fingers to discover they were split and bleeding. It only took a couple of minutes to untie his legs.

Whispering another thank you to his maker, Clay stood on his wobbly legs and tried to walk. He fell with a painful thud. Half crawling and half staggering, he fought to regain his footing. Catching his breath, he took a step. With a nod of satisfaction, he took a second, then third, thankful he still had his boots. A couple of dark shadows crossed his path. Glancing upward, he spied several vultures circling overhead.

"Sorry boys, I ain't quite done yet."

Clay trudged forward, following the trail toward Cool Water. He fell to his knees about a half-hour later, gasping for air. He squinted against the sun and closed his eyes, not believing what he saw. Shading his eyes, he took another look. A lone Indian was running toward him, followed by several people on horseback. The unmistakable figure of Teresa, mounted on her red stallion, Diablo, was on the heels of the lead rider.

Shaking his head, he collapsed face-first into the dried grass and sand.

Chapter 41

Captain Ramos sat easy in the saddle and took the lead behind Running Bird. He admired the lean frame of the youth, standing several inches taller than the rest of the Yaqui. His height compared with his body-mass was deceptive, giving an impression of weakness. Captain Ramos had made a life-long study of men, preparing them for war, and this Indian was better than most he had led into battle. Running Bird had set an even stride that carried them quickly through the brush and grassland, slowing occasionally to pick up the trail they followed. He never seemed to tire. Jose would have recruited him instantly into his regiment of Federales if he had not retired.

Jose raised his eyes from the Yaqui to survey the horizon. He raised his hand, bringing the riders to a halt as a lone figure staggered toward them. *"Santa Maria, Madre de Dios.* I don't believe it."

"What is it, captain?" Theodore said, shading his eyes against the sun.

"I think it is Clay Best."

Running Bird stopped in the distance and began waving franticly. Without hesitation, Teresa kicked Diablo in the flanks and the animal shot forward.

"By damned, I think you're right." Theodore and Jose both spurred their mounts after her, but they were no match for the stallion. Teresa leaped from the saddle and knelt to cradle Clay's head in her lap.

Jose grabbed his canteen and knelt beside her. "*Santa Maria,* they beat him badly."

"Yes, we need to get him back to the rancho," Teresa said, grabbing for the canteen.

"Go easy, *señora,*" Jose said as she poured a generous amount into Clay's mouth. "Too much water will be worse than none. Just a little every few minutes."

"Leo?" Teresa looked up with moist eyes.

"*Sí, señora?*"

"You're well mounted. Ride as quickly as you can to Carrizo Springs and bring Doctor Spencer. Julio, you go with him in case they are still out there. We will take my husband back to the rancho and be waiting for you."

Both vaqueros galloped cross country toward Carrizo Springs without a word.

"I wouldn't want to have a run-in with either of them right now," Theodore said with a chuckle. "They had a little spit in their eyes."

"They know it's war now, *Señor* Russell; said Captain Ramos. "They will do what is necessary."

Teresa sniffed and wiped her eyes against her gloved hands. "Running Bird? I want you to follow the trail and see where they are going. Take the spare horse and be careful."

"Here, take my canteen," Captain Ramos said.

The Yaqui nodded and slung the canteen over his shoulder and led the horse a few yards west. He studied the tracks a few seconds, then mounted and trotted away through the dry grass and brush.

Teresa poured another small amount of water into Clay's mouth and was rewarded with a small grin.

"God sent an angel to rescue me," he whispered with a croak.

"Shhhh, you can talk later. We need to get you home."

She looked up and sniffed as she smiled. "He will ride with me. I'll hold him and keep him from falling."

"Yes, ma'am," Theodore said with a chuckle and hoisted Clay up with his arms around Clay's chest.

"Grab his feet, captain. Ma'am? Need a hand climbing aboard behind him?"

Teresa glanced at him before leaping on Diablo and wrapping her left arm around Clay's waist. She nudged the horse forward without a word.

"I guess she doesn't need any help," Theodore said with a chuckle.

"No, *Señor* Russell, I don't believe she does."

Chapter 42

Leaving their horses at the livery with Miguel Villa. Leo strolled quickly toward Dr. Spencer's office. Julio, however, bypassed the doctor and went to Ray King's office.

In a matter of a few minutes, Sheriff King had kissed his wife and sons and strapped on his gun belt. "Be back tomorrow morning, once I find out what's going on." He kissed Maria once more and grabbed his Winchester.

Dr. Spencer was already at the stable, waiting for Miguel's sons to harness the bay to his buggy.

"I'll be needing my horse, Miguel, and won't be back until tomorrow," Sheriff King said.

"*Sí, Señor* King. Tell Teresa me and Juanita will come see them tomorrow."

"I shore will."

Julio and Leo tossed their saddles onto a couple of fresh horses and took the lead out of town. The rested animals made good time covering the ten miles to Cool Water. Dr. Spencer removed his hat before entering Clay's house, then stopped and laughed. Clay had been bathed and dressed, and was sitting at the table eating a tortilla filled with rice and beans. An empty coffee mug and another mug filled with water sat before him, as well as a cup of wine.

"I'll be damned," Dr. Spencer said as he tossed his medical bag on the table. "I doubt if anyone could hurt you with a brick."

"Oh, I hurt all right, doc. Every bone in my body hurts, especially my ribs."

"Well, let's remove your shirt and have a look-see."

Clay groaned several times as Teresa unbuttoned his shirt and slipped it off. He groaned louder as she removed the thin undershirt, revealing several ugly bruises.

"Argh! Careful, doc." Doctor Spencer pressed the bruised ribs with his finger.

"Well, I'd say you have several cracked ribs. I'll wrap you up, but it's not going to stop the pain. It's something that's just going to have to heal on its own. I'm more concerned with that cut on the top of your head. I think it needs a couple of stitches."

"Well, sew it up then, and let's get this over with."

"How much of that wine have you drunk?"

"He drank *dos* cups of wine," Teresa said, holding up two fingers.

"This is his third cup?"

"*Sí.*"

"Well, the reason I ask is," Dr. Spencer began threading a surgical needle, "I have some laudanum, but mixing it with alcohol isn't recommended. You can have a spoonful, but that's about it."

"Just stitch me up, doc. It can't hurt more'n it already does."

"I wouldn't be too sure about that."

Clay gritted his teeth and gripped the table when Dr. Spencer swabbed and cleaned the wound with a whisky-soaked rag. He also moaned and swore a few times as the doctor pulled the stitches tight. After the last stitch was tied, Dr. Spencer rinsed the needle with whisky and washed his hands.

"I'd recommend approximately two weeks of rest, to let your body heal. Whoever it was did a real job on you with their boots."

"Well, I appreciate the advice, doc, but that ain't likely."

The doctor glared at Clay and raised his voice. "If you try heavy lifting, or chasing after the man who did this, you might cause the cut on your head to fester, or even puncture a lung with a broken rib."

"Thing is, doc, I'm already festering, and someone's gotta stop James Westfall, or he's gonna keep on killing and robbing folks.

"Let Sheriff King handle stopping him. You need to heal."

"It ain't Ray's problem. With me, it's personal."

"I hate to disagree with you, knot-head. But since when isn't killing and robbing not my business? I've got a silver star here on my vest that says it is." Ray tapped the badge.

"It is, if it's done within five miles of Carrizo Springs, but this ranch is out of your jurisdiction. Besides, he came onto my ranch and nabbed me coming outa the outhouse. So, it's personal with me."

"Yeah, and I've got a hole in my back that makes it kinda personal with me too."

Ray turned away and stomped out the door where a crowd had begun to gather.

"Well, is he going to live?" Captain Ramos said, lighting a cigar.

"Hell, he's too stubborn to die. Where's that Indian guide that found him?"

"His name is Running Bird, and he's out following the trail to see where they're headed. Once we find out where they are, we thought we would tell them how much we appreciate what they did."

"Let me know when he returns. I'd like to ask him a couple of questions."

Ray went to the saloon and helped himself to a couple of glasses of Clay's better whiskey. Estrella waddled in carrying a plate of tortillas, rice and beans with shredded beef. She slid the plate in front of him with a warm smile.

"You're about to have that baby right soon, aren't you?"

"*Sí*, I wish he could come soon. I am tired and my back hurts."

"You'll forget all about that once you hold him in your arms. What kind of daddy do you think Julio is going to make?"

She stared at him thoughtfully and grinned.

"He will be a good father," she said with a nod. "People are afraid of him because he is a *pistolero,* but Julio is kind and gentle."

"Huh," Ray said and nodded slowly. "I can't wait to see that side of him. It'd be different."

******

It was late afternoon when Running Bird returned to the ranch with a lathered horse and dismounted at the stable. He first dunked this head in the watering trough and slicked his long hair back with his hands. He walked quickly toward Clay and Teresa's house dripping water. A small crowd grew in his wake. He stopped at the porch where Clay sat talking to Ray King and Dr. Spencer. Running Bird handed Captain Ramos his canteen without a word and nodded toward Clay.

"Know where they're headed, son?"

He stared blankly for a couple of seconds before scanning the crowd for Estrella. She climbed the step with difficulty and repeated Clay's question.

"He says s*í*. He will lead you when you are ready."

"Tell him much obliged. I'll make sure he gets full wages as a scout when we get back. Also tell him to get a good night's rest. We're leaving early in the morning."

Running Bird nodded as Estrella translated.

"Also, tell him I reckon he was the one that saved my life, and I'd like him to have this as a gift." He held out his personal hunting knife and sheath. It ain't much, but it's all I've got.

Running Bird held the knife gently in his hands and smiled. He turned and ran toward the Indian village.

"Well, I reckon you made an impression," Ray said. "He'll cherish that five-dollar knife like a million dollars."

"Yeah, well I wish it was a million dollar knife. I'd be coyote bait right now if it wasn't for him."

"Regardless, he's the most polite and respectful Indian I've met," Ray said as he rolled a smoke.

"How would you know? He doesn't speak or understand English?"

"It doesn't matter. I can tell. Besides, I know Spanish better than most Mexicans."

"That might be so, but how many Indians have you known?"

Ray turned to look at Doctor Spencer.

"You sure did a good job on him, Doc. He's just as ugly and disagreeable as ever. And," he turned back toward Clay, "I've known quite a few Indians in my time. Most of them disagreeable Apaches, and I shot them."

"Well, that ain't a fair comparison, now is it?"

******

Clay sat in his favorite chair on the front porch, smoking his pipe and sipping coffee. Teresa and Rob had gone all out preparing that evening's meal. He'd over-eaten, but figured it wouldn't hurt none in the long run. From where he was sitting he could see Running Bird near the corral. The boy had become some sort of celebrity and had a small crowd of Indians gathered around him. He had the knife strapped to his thigh with leather thongs. Estrella waddled across the road toward Julio who was standing in front of the saloon smoking. He figured it wouldn't be but a matter of days before she would give Julio either a son or daughter. He was conflicted on whether or not to take Julio in the morning. Estrella would want him at her side the moment she went into labor, and if by chance something went wrong and Julio didn't make it, she'd go through all kinds of hell. So would he as a matter-of-fact, knowing he'd been responsible for taking him on such a dangerous mission. But, that was the nature of things when you strapped a gun on you hip.

Clay took a sip of brandy and sucked on the pipe stem. He hoped and prayed for the day when none of them had to strap their guns on just to go out and check on the herd. Maybe someday.

Chapter 43

Running Bird chose a mutton-back black mare and rode her with a blanket instead of a saddle. He held the horse at an easy lope as he cut across the grassland, slowing to a walk at noon. He stopped on a small rise overlooking the Rio Grande four hours later. Clay reined Loco beside him, with Ray and Captain Ramos on the opposite side. Julio and Leo stopped beside Clay and rolled smokes, then sat quietly smoking.

"Huh, might of known it. Eagle Pass," Ray said with a snort. "Finding them in that mess will be like finding a snowball in Hell."

"Maybe, maybe not," Clay said. "I know Westfall like the back of my hand. He can't pass a saloon or card game when he's got a little money in his pocket." He took a swig from his canteen and swished it in his mouth before spitting.

"You said they made a pretty good haul from that last stage. So, the way I figure is, you'll find them inside one of the saloons right now."

"Yeah, but which one? There's gotta be a dozen or more."

"It won't be some fancy bar or dance hall, since they wouldn't tolerate his type. And, it won't be the worst either, since Westfall thinks highly of himself. It'll be one that ain't half bad."

He turned toward Julio and Leo.

"What do you boys think?"

"*Sí*," Leo said, tossing his cigarette butt away. "I think he's down there. Want us to go kill him for you?"

"No, not so fast," Clay said with a chuckle. "First, one of you can give Running Bird my deep appreciation, and tell him we'll join him back at the ranch in a day or two. Then, we're going down there and make acquaintance with the local law. Next, we're gonna get some chow and a good night's sleep. We'll send those highbinders to Hell sometime tomorrow morning."

Julio told Running Bird what Clay had said and received an animated reply that contained arm-waving and head shaking.

"He says he will stay. He has your knife now, which has strong magic. He will help us get the men that hurt you."

"Well ...," Clay drawled, "tell him he needs to do exactly what I say, or the deal's off. Understand?"

"*Sí*." Julio nodded and translated the command.

"He's says he will," Julio said after a minute.

"Okay, let's find the sheriff, if they've got one. Eagle Pass goes through lawmen quicker than most men change their underwear."

Clay nudged Loco toward town, dreading what lay ahead. Eagle Pass wasn't the place any decent folk would wish to spend any length of time, and the sight of the young Yaqui might cause a stir. The town had its roots sunk deep into conflict.

During the Mexican war, a company of Texas Mounted volunteers under the command of Captain John A. Veatch established an observation post on the Rio Grande. It was opposite the mouth of the Mexican Rio Escondido, near an old smuggler's trail. The crossing was known as *El Paso del Aguilar* due to the large number of Mexican eagles living in the wooded grove along the Escondido. Long after the war had ended, and the military site was abandoned, *El Paso del*

Aguilar remained a popular crossing for the trappers, frontiersmen, and traders. Fort Duncan was established two miles upstream in 1849, and a small settlement sprang up at the crossing below the post. James Campbell arrived from San Antonio and opened a trading post in 1850. He was soon joined by William Leslie Cazneau and his wife, Jane, and the village changed its name from *El Paso del Aguila* to Eagle Pass. Friedrich Groos contracted to haul supplies for the military and brought seventy Mexican families to settle near the fort. A stage line between Eagle Pass and San Antonio was established in 1851, and Our Lady of Refuge Catholic Church was built in 1852.

But while the settlement continued to grow, things weren't always pleasant and Eagle Pass became known for its violence. The village and fort were frequently attacked by Lipan Apache and Comanche Indians. Large coal deposits were discovered on the opposite bank of the Rio Grande. Piedras Negras sprang to life in 1850, and soon became a haven for fugitive slaves. Both banks of the river were infested with outlaws, killers and thieves. In 1855 James H. Callahan made a gallant, but vain, effort to curb some of the violence when he led three companies of volunteers across the river in pursuit of renegade Lipans and Kicakapoos. The Mexican government took exception to the gesture, and Callahan soon found himself in a battle against Mexican forces on the banks of the Escondido. He fell back and set the village of Piedras Negras on fire before crossing back into Eagle Pass.

Following the Civil War, bands of cattle thieves and fugitives led by John King Fisher dominated Eagle Pass. It took the aid of the Texas Rangers and the coming of the railroad in 1884, linking Eagle Pass to Galveston and San Antonio, to eventually establish law and order. Even John Fisher had gone from being an outlaw to a legitimate rancher, and even a lawman. Clay could remember seeing him once, as he strutted down the street dressed in an ornamented Mexican sombrero, a black Mexican jacket embroidered with gold, a crimson sash, and Mexican boots. He carried two silver-plated ivory-handled revolvers swinging from his hips. The man was proud as a peacock, and had silver bells attached to his spurs to attract attention. The road leading to his ranch had a sign stating: "This is King Fisher's road. Take the other." His ranch was reported to be a haven for drifters and criminals. Like most men who tried riding both sides of the law, John King Fisher came to a quick end when he and his pal Ben Thompson were gunned down inside the Vaudeville Variety Theater in San Antonio on March 11, 1884. Clay was a lawman at the time and happened to be in San Antonio. He was called upon to oversee the shipment of Fisher's body back to his ranch for burial.

The city now had a teeming population of more than 2,000, who wanted nothing more than to go on with their lives and to be left alone. They had built a courthouse and an Episcopal Church, which was the first Protestant church in the area.

The sight of the Yaqui mounted on the black horse brought a few shouts and obscene gestures as they rode down the main road toward the jail. Clay was fairly certain the only thing keeping Running Bird alive was the sight of the heavily armed men surrounding him. Leaving their horses at the livery, they made their way toward the sheriff's office. The walkway cleared, giving them a clear path as they approached. Clay opened the door and stepped inside first, with the others crowding in behind him. Texas Ranger Curtis Hart looked up from the desk and grinned.

"You were the last person I was hoping to see today."

"And why's that?" Clay said, leaning his Winchester against the wall.

"You always bring trouble wherever you go. That's why. And from the looks of your friends, I'd say you haven't changed none."

Clay felt the coffee pot and found it cold.

"Well, if you was any kind of a host, you would have made fresh coffee. I guess I'll have to make my own."

"If you remember right, that pretty Mexican woman you had last time you came made the coffee." Ranger Hart surveyed the men standing behind Clay and shook his head. "You've come down a notch, Clay. There isn't a woman among then, and none of them are pretty."

"You must mean Teresa."

"I think that was here name."

"I married her, and she just had our baby. So, she's home taking care of her."

"Her?"

"She had a beautiful baby girl," Captain Ramos said.

"That so? God help the baby. Julio I know, and I think he's Leo Santiago, if I'm not mistaken."

"That fine-looking gentleman is Captain Jose Ramos of the Mexican Federales."

"Retired," Jose said, extending his hand toward Curtis to shake.

"This here's Ray King, sheriff of Carrizo Springs, and this young man is Running Bird. He's our Yaqui guide."

Curtis gave Running Bird a nod.

"You were here in Eagle Pass last time I was here ... right in this very office. What are you doing back in here? They make you sheriff, or something?"

"Something," Curtis said and stood up to show Clay a bloody bandage on his right leg. "I happened to be in town when the new sheriff had to break up a gunfight at the Trail Dust. He took one in the shoulder and another grazed his head. He's over at the doc's now being looked after."

Clay sat in an empty chair and pulled his pipe and tobacco from his vest pocket.

"He gonna be okay?"

"Doc says he will. Young fellow, named Ben Rivers. He'll mend, but he may not want any part of the job after this." Curtis sat back down with a wince.

"What about the fellas that plugged you two?"

"They're at the undertakers. They weren't no match for a sawed-off twelve-gauge. Now, I've gotta wait until my replacement arrives in a couple of days. I don't figure you're here on a social visit. What's going on?"

"Well, we've been trailing James Westfall and Curley Hammond. They've got a vaquero with them called Carlos Mendoza. I suppose you know all about 'em."

"Yeah, I know something about them. Why? You think there here in Eagle Pass?"

"That's what this here Yaqui says. He followed their trail here yesterday."

"Dammit! I was hoping for a quiet couple of days." Curtis gripped the edge of the desk as he stood. Grabbing a crutch leaning against the wall, he hobbled toward the hat rack and retrieved his gun belt. "How'd you get involved in running him down anyway? You're supposed to be retired."

"Well, I was. But I got involved after they stuck up the bank at Lehmann's Ranch. They came into town afterward and made themselves at home in the saloon. When Sheriff King took exception, one of 'em plugged him in the back, and another shot the bartender. Me and Julio trailed them and got pretty close. But they killed an old rancher and his wife and wounded their stable hand. Me and Julio found three children inside the cabin, and figured they needed caring for. So we called off the hunt and headed home. Then, they snuck onto my ranch a couple of nights ago and whacked me on the head and dragged me off. Westfall beat the hell outa me and staked me out between a couple of mesquites. I figure someone's gotta stop them. You don't have to get involved, Curt, with that bum leg and all."

"They hell you say," Curtis laughed. "This is my town until the replacement arrives, so it's my job. Besides, I might not be much help, but I'll be damned if I'm going to miss all the fun. Ready?"

"I was hoping to get a bite to eat first."

"The Rangers will buy you a steak dinner and a nice clean room at the hotel after it's over. Come on, let's get 'er done."

"Don't you think we'd better find out where they are first?" Ray said. "Or do you wanna go limping all over town looking for them?"

"Me and Leo will find them," Julio said, reaching for the door.

"Okay, but make sure you come back here and tell us when you do. I know you two, and I don't want to have to explain to your wives how I got you killed."

Julio opened the door but slammed it shut as a bullet bit into the casing beside this head. The windows seemed to explode as a volley of gunfire erupted in the street.

"I knew it, sure as you're born," Curtis yelled. "You brought plenty of trouble with you."

"Clay!" Westfall yelled from across the street. "Clay Best. We know you're in there. You've been causing me a passel of trouble. How come you ain't dead? Don't tell me that woman of yours come along and rescued you."

Clay shook his head and chuckled. "Damn, he sure loves listening to himself talk."

"I said, how come you ain't dead?" Westfall yelled louder.

Clay aimed his .45 out the window and pulled the trigger.

"Now, that wasn't very nice, Clay. I asked a question and you shoot at me."

Clay fired again.

"That one came mighty close, Clay."

Another volley of bullets caused the men inside the jail to hug the floor.

Chapter 44

Teresa strapped the pearl-handled .38s around her hips, then placed Yolanda in the scarf tied around her neck. She walked briskly to the corral, where Diablo stood saddled and waiting. She thanked Peter Russell for saddling the horse and hitching the team to the buggy. She mounted Diablo and trotted him to where the buggy sat and smiled at several Yaqui children admiring the team. She knew Clay wouldn't like it if he knew she was going to accompany Rob and Clara Jean to Carrizo Springs, but Clay and the others might be gone several days, and she would be back long before they returned. Clara came from their room in the saloon dressed in a faded cotton dress and sunbonnet, smiling. Rob, as usual, showed little emotion. He helped Clara into the buggy, then handed her their baby tucked into a picnic basket.

"Who's going with us?" Rob asked as he climbed in and took the reins.

"No one. I know the way," Teresa said. She nudged Diablo forward, but reined him to a stop as Theodore stepped in front of the horse.

"That's not a good idea," she said with a crooked smile. "Sometimes Diablo does not stop."

"I reckon that might be true." Theodore rubbed the red stallion on the neck. "But it isn't a good idea for you three to be taking off by yourselves with all the trouble happening around us. Give me a few minutes and I'll saddle a horse and go with you."

"There's no need for you to go, *señor*. I have my guns and there's Antonio. There's also a shotgun in the buggy."

"That might be true, and you might be a crack shot with those Smith and Wessons, but Clay would skin me alive if something happened to you and that baby girl. So, hold on a few minutes."

Theodore turned away to saddle his mare and Teresa guided Diablo into his path.

"And who will look after the rancho while we are gone? You need to be here to make decisions if something happens."

"Well ..." Theodore drawled. "Why don't you stay and I'll take these young'uns to Carrizo Springs? I ain't gonna tell them something that you wouldn't like."

"I never thought you would," Teresa said with a giggle. "You know more about running a rancho than my husband and I do. So, you stay. We can take care of ourselves."

"Wait for me," Hildegarde said as she hurried toward the buggy. "There's a few things I need from the store."

She squeezed in beside Clara, placing a spare shotgun behind the seat.

"All right," Theodore stepped back, "all three of you women are more stubborn than a mule. Keep a clear eye and clear heads. Especially you, Rob. I don't want to lose most of my family."

"Yes, sir," Rob said and slapped the reins. The buggy rolled forward at a fast trot, with Teresa keeping pace.

"Why are we making this trip in the first place?" Hildegarde asked after a couple of minutes. "We probably should wait for your husband and the others to return."

"I need to tell *Señor* Johnson what is happening, and that he needs to be sheriff until *Señor* King returns. And," she added with a chuckle, "I want to see the kitchen in the *cantina* to make sure Rob has everything he needs. *Señor* Roberts may be a nice man, but he will cheat them if I don't keep watching him."

"So," Hildegarde said with a grin. "What exactly are you going to get out of all this?"

"*Porque?*"

"I mean, why are you going through all this trouble? There's got to be something in it for you."

Teresa glared at her before heaving a deep sigh.

"There is nothing for me to gain, *señora*. Only that my friends have a good job and are happy. Is that hard to understand?"

Hildegarde tilted her head back and laughed loudly.

"No, it isn't hard to understand … not in the least. Clara was wondering, and I thought she should hear it from you."

"Mama!" Clara shook her head and nudged her mother.

"Well … you did ask the question."

"We've got company," Rob said as Antonio barked loudly.

"Who?" Teresa reined Diablo around and stared. A small band of Indians were approaching quickly. Teresa slipped the thong off both pistols and pulled the right gun, letting her arm dangle to her side.

"Looks like some of those working at your ranch," Hildegarde said, shading her eyes from the sun.

"I think you may be right. Otherwise, Antonio would be growling. Wait here." She trotted Diablo toward the Indians a few yards and waited. She recognized the leader to be Grey Eagle, one of the minor chieftains. The Yaqui raised his right palm toward her as he approached.

"What are you doing here, Grey Eagle?" Teresa asked in Spanish.

"Thee-dore say we follow … keep you … others safe," he said in halting English.

"He did, did he?" she said with a grin.

"*Sí*, we go."

Teresa pranced Diablo back and forth in front of them before holstering the pistol.

"And what if I say for you and the others to go back to the rancho?'

"Thee-dore say not to listen. We go. Keep you safe."

"Well, then, I suppose if you need to keep us safe, you'd better ride closer."

She trotted back to the buggy laughing.

"What do they want?" Clara asked.

"Your papa ordered them to protect us. He also told them not to listen to me if I tell them to go home."

"Sounds like him." Hildegarde chuckled as she shook her head. "So, what happens now?"

"We go to Carrizo Springs like we planned."

"What about them?" Clara pointed toward the Yaquis.

"They are coming to protect us."

Teresa smiled and nudged Diablo in the flanks.

******

Leaving the buggy and horses at the stable, they walked briskly to the *jacale*. Rob drew two buckets of fresh water from the well. He gave one to his mother, and the second to the Yaqui. While the women fed the babies and washed away the trail dust, Rob sat on the porch talking to Antonio.

"Don't take it personally," he said with a snicker. "It's just that the women and the babies come first before us men."

The dog surprised him by lying at his side. Taking a chance, Rob stroked the animal's sweat-soaked back. Antonio lifted his head to stare at him, then lay back down, closing his eyes.

"Well, you're full of surprises. This is the first time you've let me touch you without trying to bite my hand off."

As he stroked Antonio's head, he lay back and closed his own eyes. "I'll bet you're no stranger to the whims of a woman, are you? Besides taking care of Mrs. Best, you've more'n likely got a female of your own somewhere ... maybe several wives and a bunch of pups. I've only got one, but we hope to have more. When we get to the saloon, I'll see if I can't scare something up to eat, how's that?"

He sat up as the women came from the *jacale*, looking washed and fresh as spring flowers. Clara Jean smiled at him.

"Were you talking to that dog, Rob Mayfield?"

"Maybe. Or, I could've been talking to one of the Indians. Anything wrong with it?"

"No, I was just wondering what would happen if the dog suddenly decided to answer you."

"If Antonio learned how to speak, we would all be very rich," Teresa said with a laugh. "Let's go find *Señor* Johnson, then we'll go to the *cantina* to buy something for us to eat."

"Better yet," Hildegarde said, falling into step with Teresa, "Why don't we just get something to eat at the restaurant?"

Teresa glanced at her from the corner of her eye.

"You've never eaten at the restaurant, *señora*, have you?"

"No. Is it bad?"

Teresa laughed.

"It's not very good."

******

Roy Johnson pretended to be upset about Sheriff King going with Clay in pursuit of James Westfall. Teresa simply smiled and sympathized with him. A half-hour later

194

she saw him strutting up and down the street wearing a silver-plated star. Since hiring Joseph Lincoln, there was really no need for him to be at the blacksmith shop, except to remind Joe and others that he was the owner.

Charlie Roberts looked up from filling several mugs of beer as they entered the saloon.

"Ah … excuse me. You're welcome inside anytime. Teresa, but I can't let them in," he said, motioning toward the Yaqui with one of the mugs. "They gotta wait outside."

"Really? And why is that?" She trailed her fingers across the bar and found them sticky.

"Why? 'Cause they're Indians, and Indians ain't welcome here."

"They are not going to drink any of your whiskey."

"It don't matter none. They just ain't welcome here. I didn't make the rules, Teresa. But, that's the way things are. You know that."

"*Sí*, I know a lot of things. I know my skin is just as dark as Grey-Eagle's, but he's not welcome and I am. Why is that, *Señor* Charlie? Besides, there is no one inside here to offend. I only see four people playing cards, and they haven't said a word."

Charlie heaved a deep sigh and glanced toward the card players. As much as he hated to admit it, she was right. It was Wednesday and the place was mostly empty until the stores and businesses closed their doors. Three of the players were regulars, who made their living playing cards. He had no idea who the fourth was, other than he had a quick fuse and cursed a lot.

"What can I get you?"

"Nothing. We just came to look at your kitchen and see if you have everything my friend needs, if he's going to work here. My Indian friends are here to keep me and these women safe." She smiled and shrugged. "Are you going to make them leave?"

"Okay, they can stay for now. But they gotta leave when the regulars come in, so make it snappy."

Teresa chuckled to herself as she entered the kitchen, then froze.

"Oh, my word," Hildegarde said.

"You can say that again," Clara echoed.

Teresa turned back through the door to yell at Charlie.

"*Señor* Roberts! What do you expect this young man to do with this? It hasn't been cleaned ... ever! I wouldn't let my chickens eat what's in there."

Charlie jerked back away from the bar and stammered. "Yes ... Juan cleaned it plenty good before he left."

"You've got to be joking," Hildegarde said over Teresa's shoulder. "There's grease everywhere ... even the floor's covered with grease, and dirty pans everywhere caked with crud."

"That's 'cause ol' Charlie tried to poison us a few days ago with his own cooking," Montana said as he shuffled the deck of cards.

"Really," Hildegarde said, placing her hands on her hips. "And was it any good?"

"We don't know," George said with a laugh. "He burnt his hand on a hot pan and dropped it on the floor. None of us were hungry enough to eat off the floor."

"Do you have something to write on?" Teresa said as she approached the bar.

"Sure, right here." Charlie reached under the bar to retrieve a pen and writing pad with a bottle of ink. "What for?"

"You are going to write down everything Rob Mayfield says."

Teresa turned to grab Rob by the arm and pull him to the bar.

"I want you to tell his man exactly everything you need, if you are going to work in that messy kitchen. And," she added as she turned away. "I want *Señora* Russell and *Señora* Mayfield to make sure he doesn't leave anything out."

"First of all," Clara said with disgust, "clean the place ... everything. It's horrible! I wouldn't touch a thing in there."

"Write that down, *Señor* Roberts," Teresa said as Charlie stared at Clara with a blank look.

"What? That the place needs cleaning? Any fool can see that. I thought that was the cook's job."

"It is ... when he makes the mess. And, if I'm not mistaken, you're the cook that made the mess." Teresa leaned across the bar and gave Charlie a crooked grin.

"I've been busy and ain't got time for no cleaning."

"Then, hire someone to clean it for you," Hildegarde said. "And while you're at it, you'd best have someone from the blacksmith's shop check out that stove. It doesn't look that safe, and it just might burn this place down."

Charlie wiped his brow on the bar towel and shook his head. The card players laughed as he began writing, and went back to their game. Teresa slipped behind the bar and filled four glasses with Charlie's best wine, setting three glasses in front of Clara Jean and her family. As she sat at one of the tables and checked on her baby, she watched the proceedings and sipped the wine.

Chapter 45

"You wouldn't by any chance have a back way out of here, would you?" Clay asked as the gunfire died down.

"You ever seen a jail with more'n one door?" Ray said.

"Can't say as I have."

"Well, this one doesn't neither."

Clay glanced up at Captain Ramos who was watching carefully out one of the windows.

"Got a make on where those yahoos are?"

"You'd better let me know what you've got planned," Curtis said, checking the loads in his revolver. "Remember? I don't run too good right now."

"Well, what I'm thinking is, we figure out where they are first. Then, you guys will keep 'em busy while I make a run for that alley between the saloon and the general store."

"Then what?"

"I ain't got that part figured out, yet. But most anything is better than staying cooped up in here getting shot at."

"Sounds like an excellent way to get filled with lead," Curtis said.

"Got any better ideas?"

"Well, no, but if we hang on long enough, maybe some of the townsfolk will lend us a hand."

"They might," Clay said, filling the empty chambers in his .45. "But maybe they won't. It's an excellent way for them to get killed also."

"The little gringo with a lot of hair is inside the store," Captain Ramos said.

"That'd be Curley. He's pretty fair with a rifle," Clay said with a nod. "You and Ray keep him pinned down."

"The vaquero is on the roof of the cantina," Leo said.

"Can you keep him busy?"

"I can kill him, if you want me to."

Clay glanced at Curtis who shrugged. "One less man to hang. Do it. Just wait until Clay opens the ball." Curtis pointed his rifle at the saloon.

"Jim Westfall is at the left window of the saloon. Me and Julio can send our greetings. Just don't take too long crossing the road. My Winchester only holds seven rounds."

"You let me worry about getting 'cross the street." Clay pulled back the hammer on his Winchester and gave Leo a nod.

"Let's do it."

Leo aimed his Henry at the wooden sign on the roof of the saloon and fired several times. A Winchester fell free from its owner's grasp and slid to the dusty street. A second later, Carlos Mendoza fell on his face and slid part-way, stopping with his right boot caught on the sign.

Ray and Captain Ramos both opened fire, filling the jail with acrid gun smoke. Clay burst through the door and dashed for the alley. He could see Westfall's head for a split second before it disappeared from sight as Julio and Curtis sent a spray of bullets at the window. The saloon window shattered into a million pieces as Clay dashed into the alley. He turned to see Running Bird on his heels, holding the knife.

"Get over there against the wall and stay there! "Clay yelled. "That knife ain't gonna be much help against a .45."

Running Bird leaned against the wall of the general store and grinned. The gunfire quieted for a few seconds before Curley and Westfall returned fire. Clay listened as Curley levered his rifle and fired several times. He figured the man was immediately behind the thin clapboard siding of the General store. He hit the siding with the butt of his rifle and yelled as he leaped toward the Yaqui.

"You'd best come out with your hands raised, Curley. We've got you surrounded."

The reply came in the form of two shots from Curley's rifle.

"That's what I figured."

Clay stepped back and fired waist-high at the siding and received a cry of pain, followed by a string of curses.

"You hit bad?"

"Yes, damn you. I'm gut-shot."

"I gave you fair warning. All you had to do was lay down you gun and come out with your hands raised."

"And then what? Let you hang me?"

Clay listened as the man groaned and cursed some more.

"That's what happens when you decide to become an outlaw, Curley. You should've known that right up front."

"Go to hell!"

Curley fired several more times, splintering the siding.

"No, Curley, I don't figure on going to hell. I've already saddled my bronc next to the Lord's, and don't figure I'll be switching brands. Toss your gun down now, and come out with your hands raised. I'll take you over to the doc's and see if he can't do something.

"Just so you can hang me? No thanks. I'd rather take my medicine my own self."

Clay could hear him lever another round into his Winchester. Curley groaned loudly as he flung the door wide and staggered into the street firing. He was met with a hail of gunfire that propelled him backwards. He fell halfway on the wooden walkway as his blood stained the dusty street. Clay shook his head and said a little prayer for Curley's soul, not knowing if the man really had one.

"Westfall? James Westfall? Can you hear me?"

"Yeah, I hear you fine, Clay."

The voice came from behind, sending a shiver up his spine.

"The question is, can you hear me?"

"Yeah, I hear you just fine, Jim. You ready to give up?

James laughed hard and coughed.

"Damn, but you're full of horse-manure. A better question is how long I'm going to keep you alive."

Clay felt the barrel of Jim's .45 against the back of his neck and heard the hammer cock.

"Hand me your iron, butt first."

He took Clay's pistol and stuffed it in his belt. He then pulled the extra pistol that Clay kept stuffed in his belt and tossed it.

"Rifle too. Let it fall."

Clay dropped the Winchester and raised his hands.

"Now, we're gonna cross the street and go down to the livery. You're gonna saddle two good horses. One for you, and one for me."

"Where we going?"

"Mexico. And if any of your friends try stopping us, you're gonna get the first bullet. Understand?"

"Yeah, I understand fine. But you've caused so much trouble these past few months, Ranger Hart might figure it worth my dying to put a stop to you."

"Well then, we'll just have to find out, won't we? And don't go looking for that Indian to help. He saw me coming and took off like a scared rabbit." He prodded Clay with the gun. "Get moving."

Chapter 46

"Looks like Clay's got himself into a little jam," Ray said. "Anyone got any suggestions that won't get him killed?"

The men stared out the shattered windows as James Westfall marched Clay toward the livery, making sure he was on the opposite side, using Clay as a shield.

"Wait until they leave, then follow," Julio said.

"Sounds like a plan," Ray said.

"Unless he decides to kill *Señor* Clay before he leaves," Jose said.

"We can't know that," Leo said as he rolled a cigarette. "If that happens, I'll make sure he dies real slow."

"Whatever you do, I won't be coming with you," Curtis said. "Doc says I'm not supposed to do any riding for a while. Just bring me Westfall's head, so I can tell headquarters he's for sure dead. And you wouldn't have an extra one of those, would you?" he said as Leo lit the cigarette.

"Take this one," Leo said, passing the smoke to the ranger.

"Thanks. I ran out before you guys arrived."

Leo began rolling another and peeked out the window.

"They're at the livery and are entering the barn. It is safe to follow, if we go the back way."

"Well, let's do it," Ray said and opened the door slowly.

******

Running Bird had seen the gunman rushing toward him and slipped quickly into the brush. He watched as the man had taken Clay's guns and marched him into the street. He slipped quickly between the buildings and retrieved the discarded weapons. Waiting until he thought it was safe, he ran back behind the saloon and headed quickly toward the stable. He waited until he was sure that was where they were headed, then ran hunched over past the corral and entered the back of the barn.

Laying the guns in a pile of hay, he hid inside a horse stall. It was only a matter of a minute before Clay entered with his hands raised. The gunman still had the pistol pointed toward the back of his head.

"Okay toss saddles on a couple of good horses. Make it quick!" James laughed as he stepped back, still pointing the gun at him.

"How about saddling that black of yours? I'll take him."

"Okay, if that's what you want. But he's pretty played out."

"Yeah, your right," he said, eyeing the stallion. "But I'm pretty fair at picking horseflesh, so make 'em good ones."

Running Bird slipped quietly from the stall and inched his way toward the men. He was almost on them when the horse inside the stall next to him whistled and kicked the gate loudly. James turned to see what was happening and Running Bird sprang forward, burying his head into James' chest.

James fell against a stall and swung the .45 toward the Yaqui, but his shot went wild as Clay clubbed him with a saddle. Clay lunged toward him and grabbed his wrist.

Westfall proved himself surprisingly strong, and the searing pain in Clay's ribs reminded him he was far from having mended. Running Bird danced around them, hoping to find an opening where he could use the knife. Westfall grabbed Clay's left wrist, twisting it in order to point the pistol at him. Clay swung his right fist, hitting Westfall's face twice with little effect.

"Damn, but you've lost a lot since or last fight," James said with a laugh, and twisted his wrist harder.

Clay's right hand found the .45 tucked into Westfall's belt and jerked it free. Westfall's eyes grew wide with the realization, and he grabbed for Clay's right arm as he pulled the trigger. The bullet took him in the stomach.

Westfall tried desperately to swing his right hand toward Clay, but Clay fired twice more, hitting him in the chest. Westfall's gun fell from his grasp as a commotion erupted at the far end of the barn.

Clay turned as Julio and Leo burst into the barn, with Ray and Jose at their heels. They were soon followed by a crowd of townspeople, all crowding the windows and doors, hoping to see what was going on.

"Well, I reckon that'll do it. We can go home now," Ray said, staring at the body.

"Yes, we can," Clay said. It ain't that I don't like y'all, but I'm ready for one of Teresa's meals, a hot bath and a soft bed.

"Amen," Ray said.

Running Bird tried handing Clay the knife as he spoke rapidly.

"He says the knife's magic didn't help him this time. He again thanks you for giving it to him, but it must be your knife," Julio said.

"Tell him he is wrong. Tell him it was his charging at Westfall that distracted him enough for me to do what I did. It is his knife now, and it's magic will grow stronger, if he uses it for good."

"Well, you boys wanna lend me a hand?" Ray said. "Curt said he wants Westfall's head so he can tell ranger headquarters he's dead. I ain't into cutting heads off, so let's just give him Westfall's whole danged body."

"That'll do," Clay said, patting Running Bird on the back. "Then we'll check into the hotel and get something to eat. I'd like to head home before first light tomorrow."

Chapter 47

Charlie Roberts was busy restocking the liquor bottles behind the bar when the doors swung open.

"We're closed," he said loudly.

"I know you are, *Señor* Roberts," Teresa said.

"Oh, you again," he said with a groan. It had been two days since she had highjacked him into agreeing to pay for a bunch of expensive pots, pans and kitchen utensils. He was still fuming about the cost. Juan had run the kitchen for a year without needing half the things she had on her list.

"Yes, me again. Teresa crossed the room and stopped shy of the bar. Rob and his mother-in-law entered, carrying several pots and pans. "We were planning on opening the kitchen today. If it's not convenient, we can leave."

"No, no," Charlie said. "Today's just fine, as long as I'm not supposed to buy anything else."

"No, *Señor* Charlie. We brought everything we need." She turned toward the kitchen and then stopped.

"The kitchen is clean?"

"Yes, I hired a couple of women like you suggested, and they spent a whole day cleaning. And Joe at the blacksmith's shop cleaned the flume on the stove and made a few repairs. It's like new."

Teresa opened the door and peeked inside the kitchen, then looked back at him with a smile.

"*Bueno, Señor* Charlie. It is the way a kitchen should be."

"Well, I'm glad you approve." Charlie gave a crooked scowl and shooed at them with his bar towel. "Now, go on, do what you do and leave me alone."

"Oh, one more thing," Hildegarde said over her shoulder.

"I knew it," Charlie said. "What is it now?"

"We explained to the man at the market what we were doing, and he said we could buy what we needed, and he would bill you weekly."

"You what? My lord woman! You're going to drive me into the poorhouse."

"Don't worry so much, *Señor* Charlie. You will more than make up what we spend long before the night is over. I promise," Teresa said with a giggle.

"We'd better. If not, I'm holding you responsible," Charlie growled.

Teresa poured herself a cup of coffee and sat at one of the tables, sipping the hot liquid as Rob, Clara and Hildegarde set the kitchen up. She checked on Yolanda, then took another sip and frowned. The coffee was another thing that needed to be improved.

She removed the telegram she had received yesterday and unfolded it on the table. The letters themselves didn't mean much, since she had never gone to public school and learned to read and write. It was Clara Jean that had read the telegram.

"Well, what does it say?" Clara had asked. The Mexican lad had ridden a lathered horse into Cool Water late in the afternoon, causing Teresa's heart to pound with fear.

"I don't know." She shook her head as a tear trickled down her cheek. "I ... I never learned how."

"Really?"

Teresa nodded.

"Then I can teach you." She took the telegram from Teresa as a crowd began to circle them. She scanned it quickly before reading it out loud.

James Westfall, Curley Hammond and Carlos Mendoza dead. Stop. All posse members well. Stop. Heading to Carrizo Springs tomorrow. Stop.

Theodore had tried vainly to talk her into waiting for Clay at Cool Water instead of riding into Carrizo Springs, then gave up when she threatened to shoot him. She hugged and kissed Clara Jean repeatedly on the cheek.

"*Gracias, Señora. Gracias* for reading that to me. I know you do not like living at Cool Water very much, but I wish you to stay. I need you. I need you to teach me things I cannot do. And I love you so much. You have become a dear friend to me. Please stay ... in Carrizo Springs at least."

Clara backed away, then slowly smiled. She had hated the woman standing before her with a passion only a few months ago and treated her poorly, to say the least. Now Teresa was calling her a dear friend, and begging her to stay.

"Yes. If this restaurant works out, I'm sure we will stay, not in Cool Water, mind you." She laughed and shook her head. "I'm sorry, but there's nothing here."

"I know," Teresa nodded, "but we will have a nice rancho someday."

"I believe you will have a nice place. And when that time comes, I'll be happy to spend time here, but not just now." She leaned close to whisper in Teresa's ear.

"Rob doesn't know that I know the bed we've been sleeping in was used by a saloon girl to entertain men, but I'm not that dumb."

Teresa laughed and kissed her cheek.

"No, you're not *estúpido, señora.* But sometimes it is to our benefit to let our men think we are."

Teresa set her coffee mug on the table as Clara Jean came from the kitchen to hand her William, who was asleep in a wicker basket.

"He's finally asleep. Would you mind watching him while I help mama and Rob with the kitchen?"

"I would be happy to."

The remainder of the day seemed to drag as the hands of the mantle clock on the shelf behind the bar moved slower and slower. She had finally decided the blasted thing must be broken when the aroma of spicy beef and chiles drifted from the kitchen to assault her nostrils.

"By damned, whatever they are cookin' shore smells good," Frank said as he shuffled a fresh deck of cards.

"I agree with Frank, which ain't very often," George said. "When are they gonna let us sample the grub?"

"I don't know. Whenever they get it done, I reckon," Charlie said.

It was only a matter of minutes before Clara came from the kitchen to slide a plate of rice, beans and a flour tortilla filled with spiced beef and onion onto the table. The men immediately abandoned their card game to crowd around Teresa's table.

"Back off boys," Clara said. "Mrs. Best needs to sample this before any of you can get yours."

"Please make it snappy, ma'am," Frank said. "My stomach is beginning to think my throat's been cut."

Teresa took her time sampling the rice and beans, before taking a bit of the tortilla. She chewed thoughtfully, allowing the flavor to settle on her taste buds. She swallowed and smiled.

"Tell *Señor* Rob it is perfect."

"Ya hear that, Charlie? Tell him to bring it on," Frank yelled.

"I guess we're in business," Charlie said.

Clara hurried toward the kitchen with a smile.

"Tell him I want a plate just like the one Mrs. Best is eating!" Frank yelled after her. "We all do."

"You haven't heard how much it costs," Charlie said.

"Well, how much?" George said.

"I don't know yet. I need to talk to Rob and see what it's costing me."

"Here, *Señor* Roberts," Teresa said, handing him a folded piece of paper. "I think this might be a fair price for the food they are cooking."

Charlie unfolded and read the paper, then nodded.

Charlie's Cantina
Bill of Fare

Coffee and bread, or tortilla, ... 5 cts.
Tortilla ....5 cts.
Beans ...., ... 5 cts.
Rice ....5 cts.
Tortilla with beef ....10 cts.
Complete meal ....20 cts.

"That does not include what you sell from the bar." she said with a grin.

"Is it enough?"

"I believe so. I will have Rob give you a complete list with prices when we see how this goes."

"Here's the bill of fare, boys." Charlie passed the paper around.

"Here, *hombres*," Teresa held out a forkful of spicy beef toward Frank. "Take a taste."

Frank closed his eyes as the flavor assaulted his taste buds. The others stared as he swallowed.

"Well?" Montana said.

"I don't care what it costs," Frank said. "Bring it on!"

Charlie grinned as he took each man's money, then marched to the kitchen to place their orders.

Teresa smiled at William as he stirred inside the basket with a whimper.

"You may not know this, little *señor*, but your papa is going to be a wealthy business man."

Chapter 48

Noon arrived with a rush as word began to spread that the kitchen inside Charlie's Cantina was now open and serving mouth-watering Mexican dishes. Teresa had to wait tables for an hour, carrying Yolanda, while Clara took William to the *jacale* to feed him.

"I think Rob is going to have to hire someone to wait tables," Clara said on her return. "I had no idea it would be this busy."

"Oh, *Señora* Mayfield," Teresa said with a laugh, "you have no idea how busy it will get."

"It'll get busier?"

"Much more, especially on Saturday, when people come to town to buy supplies, and *vaqueros* come to drink and gamble. You will be working much harder."

Clara stared at her, open-mouthed, and shook her head.

"You will also need to hire kitchen help. You will need someone to wash and clean and help Rob while he prepares food. Your mother can't work every day like this."

"Won't that mean he'll make less money? You know what a skinflint that old man behind the bar is."

"Maybe, a little at first. But you simply raise the price of a meal a few pesos. They will still buy his food."

******

Teresa went to the *jacale* with the intention of feeding Yolanda and lying down, but resting seemed impossible. Every time she closed her eyes, she saw Clay and the others riding lathered horses across the desert, but never drawing closer.

She paced the dirt floor, rocking and singing softly to her baby, before kneeling before the wooden crucifix her grandfather had carved from a dead mesquite when she was a small girl. Tears spilled over as she prayed to the Holy Father to keep her husband and his companions safe. She ended the prayer by vowing she would dedicate her precious Yolanda to the Holy Church, perhaps as a nun, then laughed, knowing the final decision would be Yolanda's.

She paced the floor again, stopping momentarily to kiss her sleeping daughter's head and inhale her scent. She stared out the door and down the wide street as heat waves danced in the distance. The light breeze seeping through the reed thatched walls kept it tolerable inside. A red-tailed hawk circled overhead, casting its shadow across the roadway as he looked for a midday meal.

She returned to her pacing as Antonio watched from his vantage point in the corner. It was mid-afternoon when he barked at several dusty riders as they rode their lathered horses to Miguel's stable. Teresa watched from the doorway as they dismounted, then darted toward one particular rider as he began swatting dirt from his clothing with a battered hat.

She flung herself at him, causing Yolanda to waken with a howl.

"Easy there, woman. Don't cripple our daughter," Clay said with a laugh.

"Oh, don't ... laugh at me ... I was worried ... sick," she said between kisses.

"Well, let me wash a little of this grime off my face and I'll tell you all about it."

"There is no time. I'll bathe you later. Right now, I just want to be with you."

"In that case," he scooped her off her feet and began carrying her toward Charlie's Cantina, "You'll have to buy me a beer to wash some of this dust down my gullet.

"I don't want to share you with anyone. I want you all to myself."

"I've got to give my report to Roy. He's the acting sheriff."

"No, Ray can do that. He's the real sheriff."

"I think she's got you on that one," Ray said with a chuckle. "But, I think it can wait until tomorrow," he added as Maria and his twin sons ran toward them with squeals.

"Yeah, I reckon it can wait," Clay said, kissing her on the lips.

Chapter 49

Clay leaned forward as Teresa scrubbed his back with a soapy wash cloth.

"Mmm, that feels real good."

"If you think this feels good, just wait. I have something that will feel much better."

Clay glanced at her sideways with a crooked grin.

"Hush that kinda talk, woman. Our daughter's lying in the next room, and can hear every word."

"I doubt she understands much, *marido muy fuerte*. Besides, there will come a day she will do the same for her husband."

"Huh, earlier this evening you said you had dedicated her to the church as a nun. Wouldn't that be a mortal sin?"

"Maybe, if she becomes a nun."

She cocked her head to one side and slipped her hand under the water to rub his chest.

"She might not want to be a nun. It will be her choice."

Clay caught his breath as she continued exploring.

"How's this gonna work? There's a million folks hanging around this house."

"Ah, your loving wife has taken care of that."

"Really? How so?"

"I rented a room at the hotel for Rob and Clara, and another for one for Clara's mother. I told my Yaqui guards that we wanted to be alone. They are guarding the house and won't let anyone bother us."

"Hmm, not only is my wife beautiful, she's smart as well."

Teresa quit exploring to pour two glasses of wine.

"Yes, she is beautiful and smart. She was smart enough to marry the best husband in Texas. Even his name is Best."

She kissed him then stepped back to sip her wine.

"Come, my strong handsome husband," she pulled the curtain separating the bath from the bedroom, "and I'll show you how clever I am."

"Toss me a towel."

Teresa gave him the towel and shook her head.

"There is no need for a towel. Just dry your feet."

"Really?"

"Really."

Teresa unbuttoned her dress and let it fall. She wasn't wearing any unmentionables.

"Lord have mercy," Clay said as he climbed out of the tub, dripping water on the reed mat. He dried his feet vigorously as Teresa backed toward the bed, smiling.

Chapter 50

"He's one proud peacock," Clay said with a chuckle as Roy Johnson strutted down the street making his afternoon rounds. "Bet he shines that star every day."

"Twice a day from what I hear," Ray said. It was now two weeks since they returned from Eagle Pass to a hero's welcome. The hoopla had died down, but the events leading to the killing of James Westfall, Curley Hammond and Carlos Mendoza had been branded in Clay's mind forever. The men were seated on Ray's front porch, enjoying the afternoon breeze.

"What made you decide to quit being a lawman," Clay said.

"Same reason as you ... I guess. Got tired of seeing Maria and the boys suffer, wondering if I was gonna come home."

"Roy almost gave the badge back last night," Maria said with a laugh as she poured more coffee.

"Really? How come?"

"Jason Biggs got blind-staggering drunk in Charlie's place and started making a ruckus. When Roy went to lock him in a cell to sleep it off, Jason puked all down the front of him. Said he didn't bargain for that kind of deal." Ray laughed, spilling some of his coffee.

"Huh, that sort of comes with the territory, don't it?" Clay said. "So, what've you got planned now that you're not sheriff?"

"Don't know." Ray raised his eyebrows and chuckled. "Guess I need to think of something, or we'll starve to death."

"*Sí*," Maria said with a grin. "Besides, this house belongs to Carrizo Springs for the sheriff to live in. We need to move soon so Roy and his wife can move in."

"Roy's already got a house. He said we can stay here as long as we want."

"*Sí*, but the house does not belong to Roy. It belongs to the town." She returned to the kitchen with a chuckle.

"Well, anyway," Clay said, stretching his arms, "Teresa and me talked things over, and we decided it's about time to make another trip to Mexico, and we sort of expected you might want to come with us."

"Who's *we*?"

"There'll be me, Captain Ramos, maybe Leo or Julio. I'd like one of them to say at Cool Water while we're gone, just in case something happens. I don't expect any trouble, but you never know. Four of us who know how to handle a gun should be enough, especially having the captain along. He knows that part of the country like the back of his hand."

"Huh, I kind of thought you might be joshing about going back down there when you didn't mention it again."

"No, I was dead serious about it. We've been sort of busy the past few days."

"You think there's enough left to go after?"

"Just as much as we brought back last time ... maybe more."

"Huh," Ray said thoughtfully. "I've been hoping to buy a place of our own and settle down." He studied Maria as she came from the kitchen with a plate of cookies.

"When do you plan on going?"

"I'd like to leave early next week. The weather's going to start turning cold pretty soon, and the way I figure, this drought's going to break someday. I don't particularly like riding in the rain."

"What are we going to need?"

"We've got all that figured out. Just bring extra clothes and your guns. You might throw in some extra ammo. Hopefully, we won't need it, but it's better to be prepared. Are you in?"

"Well, most of it's going to be up to Maria," Ray said thoughtfully.

"*Sí*," Maria said with a nod. "If it will get you out of that dangerous job ... go. We'll be okay while you're gone."

"You will come and stay with us at Cool Water while they are gone," Teresa said.

"Thing is, it ain't exactly going to be safe getting that gold and bringing it back," Clay said with a snicker.

Maria stared at him as he took a sip of coffee.

"You did it before."

"Sure we did, but we also had to fight our way back across the border. I don't expect any trouble, but you can never tell."

They sat in silence, staring at one another. Clay finished his coffee and leaned forward.

"Well? Are you in, or out? We've got a lot of work in the next few days if we're gonna leave Monday."

Ray studied Maria for a few seconds.

"I won't go unless it's okay with you and the boys."

"Go," she said softly. "I can't worry more than I did while you were chasing those men that shot you."

"Okay, it's settled then. I'm in."

Clay stood and leaned to kiss Maria on the forehead. "We'll take good care of him. I promise."

End

About The Authors

MAJOR MITCHELL (pictured on the left), is the author of ten historical westerns and two children's books. He lives with his wife, Judy, in Northern California.

JERRY MITCHELL (pictured on the right), is the author of several short stories, a book of poetry and co-author of four historical westerns. He lives in Northern California, approximately 25 minutes from his brother Major.

Other Clay Best Novels By These Authors

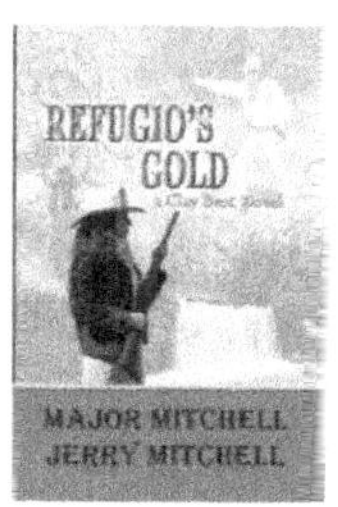

Available Now At:
www.shalakopress.com